SUSAN FARRIS

Taken For Granted
Midnight Bluff Book Two

First published by SF Consulting 2022

Copyright © 2022 by Susan Farris

All rights reserved. No part of this publication may be reproduced, stored or transmitted in any form or by any means, electronic, mechanical, photocopying, recording, scanning, or otherwise without written permission from the publisher. It is illegal to copy this book, post it to a website, or distribute it by any other means without permission.

This novel is entirely a work of fiction. The names, characters and incidents portrayed in it are the work of the author's imagination. Any resemblance to actual persons, living or dead, events or localities is entirely coincidental.

For more information about this work or the author, email susan@susanfarris.me

First edition

ISBN: 978-1-7364523-7-0

This book was professionally typeset on Reedsy. Find out more at reedsy.com

Contents

Taken For Granted	v
Also By Susan E. Farris	vi
Dedication	vii
More Stories!	viii
Taken For Granted	ix
Prologue	1
Chapter 1	6
Chapter 2	11
Chapter 3	15
Chapter 4	22
Chapter 5	29
Chapter 6	39
Chapter 7	45
Chapter 8	54
Chapter 9	61
Chapter 10	72
Chapter 11	77
Chapter 12	89
Chapter 13	97
Chapter 14	102
Chapter 15	116
Chapter 16	132
Chapter 17	136
Chapter 18	143

Chapter 19	157
Chapter 20	162
Chapter 21	170
Chapter 22	178
Chapter 23	185
Chapter 24	196
Chapter 25	212
Epilogue	217
How To Leave A Review	222
Mayor Patty's Lemon Bars	223
Acknowledgments	225
About the Author	226

Taken For Granted

Also By Susan E. Farris

The Gravedigger's Guild

Nuts About You
Taken For Granted

Heartwork

Dedication

For Pete
for always pushing me to be my best
even when I don't believe in myself.

More Stories!

Want to see more from Susan E. Farris? Receive a free Midnight Bluff bonus story (or two!) when you subscribe to Susan Farris' newsletter and be the first to hear about new books.

Head to https://susanfarris.me/subscribe/ to sign up.

Taken For Granted

Susan E. Farris

Midnight Bluff Book Two

Prologue

Sunlight glanced, hard and sparkling, off the polished blond pews of Midnight Bluff Baptist Church. Grant sniffed, his head foggy with Benadryl and the hundred different perfumes and colognes assaulting his nasal passages. What was with the people in this town and their incessant need to bathe in eau de parfum? The two Benadryl he'd taken before coming weren't even putting a dent in his allergies.

He side-eyed the floret affixed to the end of the pew at his elbow. Cress had gone all-out with the decorations. Flowers festooned every pew, window ledge, the top of the piano, and the pièce de résistance: a gigantic arch that looked like it had been whisked here from a fairy tale, covered completely in velvety roses and baby's breath.

Where in the world she had found that many roses in December was beyond him.

Just the sight of it all made his eyes water. Quietly, he pulled a tissue from the pack he kept eternally in his pocket since coming to this God-forsaken backwater and blew his nose. An awkward honk echoed through the polite chit-chat. A hundred eyes turned and pinned him to the pew, tissue frozen over his nose. He squirmed like a worm on a hook until one by one they turned back around, leaving him alone in his stuffy-headed misery.

Out of everyone in this sanctuary, he had the least business being here, and yet Leora had made it clear that she expected his attendance.

"After all," she said with a sly smile in the courthouse vestibule two weeks ago, "We must let bygones be bygones. Show this town we're bigger than our pasts." She patted his arm like they were old friends.

He'd heard himself muttering, "Of course," and knew he'd regret it until he could put this town behind him. That woman frightened the bejeezus out of him. Besides Mayor Patty, Leora McBride was the single citizen most capable of compromising everything he'd come here to accomplish.

His eyes flashed to the double doors at the back, cheeks heating. Besides winning Cress back. But that ship was sailing—had sailed— the moment she'd shoved him away and stomped his heart into the dirt.

For the last two weeks, he'd had a rancid case of heartburn and broke out into a sweat every time he saw the scallop-edged invitation stuck to his fridge. Thank God, the worst part would be over after today. He tugged his jacket straight and sat up tall. No way in heck was he going to let these people see him sweat.

Mayor Patty turned around in her pew, her coiled and crimped hair fluttering with the movement, and pressed something into his hand. Looking down, he recognized one of her handkerchiefs, her mayoral "seal" embroidered in one

Prologue

corner. Her dark eyes twinkled kindly at him. "I think you need this more than I do, darlin'." She patted his knee.

Such a small gesture. Suddenly, he felt a little less alone in this sea of whispering people. A knot formed in his throat as he croaked out, "Thank you." With a smile, she murmured, "Of course," and turned back around to nod at something her husband was saying.

With a jolt, the piano thumped out "Here Comes The Bride" and they all hushed and rose to their feet, silk and linen rustling. An exhale rushed through the crowd as the back doors burst open, and Grant clutched the arm of the pew.

Cress walked towards him, beaming, clad in an ivory silk gown that perfectly hugged her curves before flaring out at the knees. Light haloed around her, brushing her cheeks, and highlighting their ecstatic glow. She floated towards him on her grandfather Bo's arm.

He watched her glide on past, her eyes never once flicking to his face. The effort of holding himself back from reaching for her made his lungs constrict and burn. His jaw throbbed and his teeth ached as he forced his face to relax before any prying eyes could find him as they took their seats. The worst was over; there was no doubt in his mind.

She didn't love him. She didn't even know he existed anymore. He just had to endure a few more minutes, congratulate Leora, and then he could slip away and get back to work.

The sooner he could get out of this town the better.

* * *

Across the aisle, Ellie smoothed out her dress as she stood, delighted by how the satin shimmered in hues of amethyst and mauve. "Thank you for letting me borrow this," she whispered to Lou Ellen. "I don't have anything half as nice."

Lou Ellen squeezed her arm. "You know I always like dressing my foster-sister up."

Ellie chuckled as she turned back to watch Cress float dreamily down the aisle, a vision in her ivory mermaid dress. A pang ran through her as she watched Bo pat Cress' hand fondly, then hand her to Jake with a kiss and a wink. One day, she would be the one at the altar. If any of the eligible men in this town ever noticed her behind the "Land For Sale" signs. She sighed.

Pastor Riser motioned for them to sit, and as they shuffled back down into their spots, a flap of white in the corner of her eye caught Ellie's attention. Glancing over, she saw— Gill... Gary... Grant? — the man that Mayor Patty had hired to "help" the town, snapping out a handkerchief and rubbing at his nose. And he was Cress' ex that had made the big scene at the dove hunt last fall!

She tapped Lou Ellen's leg and pointed. "This must be hard for him."

Lou Ellen settled her shoulders back and floofed the ends of her hair. "If he had any decency, he wouldn't have come at all. Leave poor Cress alone."

"I'm sure he got an invitation just like everyone else. The whole town is here." Ellie craned her neck to take in the packed sanctuary. She should catch up with Mr. Monroe after the ceremony about that back forty acres he'd mentioned wanting to sell.

"Still, it's just not decent. Coming to your ex's wedding. Downright tacky." Lou Ellen raised a perfectly groomed brow.

Prologue

Mrs. Emma Jean Hicks shot them a look. They'd better hush before she turned around and smacked them with her fan like she used to do in Sunday school.

Ellie glanced back at Grant's pale face and sweaty brow. He looked like he was going to keel over any minute. She dropped her whisper even lower. "Well, I think it's kinda nice: being big enough to face the whole town to come wish your ex well."

Lou Ellen shrugged with a smile. Ellie knew they hardly ever saw eye-to-eye on these things, and it's what they liked about each other, their different perspective. As Pastor Riser pronounced "You may now kiss the bride," they whooped and clapped together.

Clutching her hand, Lou Ellen promised, eyes misty, "One day, that's going to be us up there. My daddy will walk us both down the aisle in a big double wedding." Ellie nodded, too choked up to speak. She hoped that day got here soon. She was ready for a family of her own.

Chapter 1

Grant snatched his head up off the table, jerking a searing knot into his neck. Grumpily, he prodded at the sore spot with the fingers of one hand while he studied the separated milk floating atop his cold coffee. Drat! That had been the last of the rather questionable milk.

He braced himself for the dreaded prospect of going out in public. With no rentals available in Midnight Bluff, Renewzit had taken an apartment for him in Cleveland when he'd come here over a year ago. But word spread fast in the Mississippi Delta.

And no one in *this* blasted town seemed to like him either. He'd yet had to make a single real friend. Sure, the people he saw regularly would say "hello" with a smile, but then they scurried away before he could form a response. You would have thought he had bad breath or something.

He ran his tongue over his fuzzy teeth. Ok, right now he did have bad breath. He hadn't exactly felt the spiffiest since Cress' wedding. But who could blame him? He'd embraced

Chapter 1

work as a needed distraction. So what, if his personal hygiene wasn't at its best!

In the dim light, he stared at the mess of papers scattered across the dining room table. So much information and all of it felt useless. What good did crop yields for the last twenty years do him when the heart of Midnight Bluff was dying? All anyone wanted to talk about was the glory days of the old catfish plant. But it was a relic, long-defunct—a safety hazard best torn down and sold for scrap.

He plunked his head back down on the table. With nothing new to show the mayor beyond some facade updates and a wireframe for a website, his meeting tomorrow was going to tank.

He had been stumped for months. Ever since Cress' wedding.

How had this project slipped sideways? The research stage had gone swimmingly— in a few months, he'd pulled all the records, analyzed them, double checked the zoning codes and provisions, and met with the council members to get approval for his temporary contract. Every box ticked.

Albeit things with Cress hadn't gone the way he'd intended. He rubbed at his temples as he remembered again how much of an idiot he'd been, just barreling into her life. Like all he had to do was snap his fingers and she'd come back…

That was the root of his problem. He was spending so much time dwelling on the past, he couldn't see the future. His back ached, reminding him he'd been sitting all day and that he should go for a run, pronto.

Below him, the floor of his apartment rattled as the garage door came to life. The Tisdales, his landlords, must be home from church.

Rising stiffly, he peered through the blinds, squinting against the crystal March sun. As the last of the blond-headed children disappeared inside, Mr. Tisdale glanced up toward his window. Grant froze.

The last thing he wanted was a knock on the door and then to be trapped on his doorstep for an hour while Mr. Tisdale talked about the latest happenings at the University and angled for an invitation inside. With a blink, Mr. Tisdale turned and went inside.

Grant let the slat of the shade fall back into place, relieved. Glancing around the spartan apartment, he belatedly realized the only light was emanating from his laptop screen and the light above the sink.

With a grunt, he pulled on a clean-ish pair of slacks and went to brush his teeth. It was time to find sustenance. Man couldn't live on black coffee alone.

* * *

Grant stood pondering the milk options in Vowell's. Among the two percent, whole milk, and creamer, he couldn't remember what he'd grabbed last time. He hated having to decide on little things like this; Cress had always known so much better than him what was good.

Someone tapped his shoulder. "Excuse me." A pert brunette swished by him and grabbed a half-gallon of whole milk. He blinked in recognition as Lou Ellen Pearce looked up at him, brandishing the jug. "Prairie Farms is the best around here. If that's what you're wondering."

She brushed past him again before he could say "thank you"

Chapter 1

and disappeared down the baking aisle. He shook his head and grabbed a half-gallon of the Prairie Farms as she'd suggested. Lou Ellen had bopped into the courthouse to bring her daddy, who worked down in records as the Municipal Clerk, lunch a few times.

He glanced back toward the baking aisle, wondering what Lou Ellen liked to bake. Maybe it was time to get back out there, find someone who was more in tune with him, could appreciate the things he liked.

Absentmindedly, he browsed down the coffee section, looking for something caramelly. Just as he reached for an interesting-looking bag, he spotted Lou Ellen again, looking at the jams and jellies.

There was no time like the present. Dropping the coffee in his basket, he strolled over to her. "I took your advice."

She looked up at him, confused, clutching a jar of raspberry jam. "What?"

"About the milk." He pointed at the jug sweating in the bottom of his hand basket. "I just wanted to say thank you."

"Oh." She stood gawking at him, turning the jam jar around in her hand. Crackling muzak played over the grocery store's speakers as Grant took a breath. He'd done this before—with Cress. Seven years ago. But still, it wasn't that hard. He just had to get the words out there.

"So, umm. You seem thoughtful. I'd love to take you out for coffee sometime and get to know you better. Would tomorrow be good for you?"

Lou Ellen laughed, her brows quirking together and a flush rising to her cheeks. "Oh, oh no! This is not happening." She shook her head, her hair brushing her cheeks. "My daddy would disown me for dating a Yankee."

Grant bristled. "I'm from Wisconsin! —"

Cutting him off, she waved a hand. "Same difference around here." She set the jam down on the shelf and crossed her arms. "Sweetie, I'm sorry, but look at you. You look like you just came off a bender. You're *clearly* still hung up over Cress. And you have OUTSIDER written all over you—I mean you don't even say 'sir' or 'ma'am'." With a shrug, she continued, "Are you even planning on sticking around after you do… whatever… it is that Patty wants you to do?"

He stared at her speechless, his grip tightening painfully on the basket.

She shook her head and took a step back. "Honey, get yourself figured out before you go asking anyone out again." With a wave, she disappeared around the corner.

Grant gaped at the spot she'd been. A bender? Then he looked down at himself. His jeans had a mysterious dark stain on them; his Polo was helplessly wrinkled, having been abandoned in the dryer for days. And he could only guess how bad his stubble and his—he belatedly realized—uncombed hair must look. Muttering curses, he headed for the personal care aisle. When he got home, he'd go for that overdue run then spend some quality time in the shower.

Lou Ellen was right. It was time he got his act together.

But still, did she have to laugh at him?

Chapter 2

Sweat worked its way down Ellie's back as she leaned against a tree and pulled a sip from her water bottle. If there was one thing she'd learned in her five years of selling real estate out in the Delta, it was always come prepared.

And clients don't like it if you pass out from heat exhaustion. You'll probably lose the sale.

Taking one more swig, she turned back to rejoin her client who seemed to be delighting in inspecting the barbed-wire fences that ran around Mr. Monroe's back forty acres.

"These are perfect!" he called to her. She smiled and waved back just as her phone rang.

"I'll just be one sec. Gotta get this!" As she tapped the button, she lowered her voice. "Make it quick Lou Ellen. I'm with a client."

"Oh! You will NOT believe who just asked me out in Vowell's—by the jelly, no less! Didn't even have the decency to wait until I was in flowers and produce." Lou Ellen's voice went high and breathless, a sign that she was still at Vowell's, powerwalking through the parking lot. "And he was such a mess too. All rumpled and unwashed looking."

"Lou Ellen!" She cut in before her best friend could tell her the story without telling her the story—or the guy's name. "Who was it, sugar?"

"Grant! I was just telling you." She huffed and the slam of a car door echoed over the line. "He asked me out at Vowell's. I told him what milk to get, and he took it as some sort of sign that I was into him." She babbled, "I'm sorry, but do I have a sign that says 'easy' on my forehead? No! So don't ask me out in a grocery store. So unromantic."

Ellie rolled her eyes. Lou Ellen was in her feelings now; she might have to hang up to get her off the phone. "What does that have to do with him asking you out?"

"Oh! He looked gross— all rumpled and greasy hair. And he stood there looking all shocked that I said no." She sighed. "I dunno. It was just kinda pathetic."

"Lou Ellen…" Ellie measured her words. "Did you politely tell him 'no' or did you give him one of your speeches about all the things that's wrong with him?"

Silence crackled over the line. "Ummm…."

"Lou Ellen! We've worked on this. You probably crushed the poor guy."

"Ok, first of all. He's not some 'poor' guy. He works for a big corporation, not my Uncle Ray's Gun & Tackle, and he probably has gobs of money. And second, he clearly has issues he needs to work on. I did him a favor."

"Lou-Lou." Ellie groaned "We've talked about this. It's not your job to be someone's shrink. You do you, and let other people worry about themselves."

A dramatic sigh sent a loud burst of static into Ellie's

Chapter 2

eardrum. "Why-y-y do you always have to be so…"

"Right?"

"I was going to say uptight."

Ellie blew a raspberry. "Look, I gotta go. Give Martha and Don my love."

As she hung up, Ellie brushed a sweaty strand of hair out of her eyes and sighed. Poor Grant. Having to watch his ex-girlfriend get married, then working up the guts to ask a girl out and getting turned down. That guy had it rough. She rubbed at her nose, feeling bad. Lou Ellen's little "pieces of advice" could sting.

Still, she needed to take her own advice and mind her business. She turned back to her client with a smile. "If you like the fences, you're going to love the pond back here. Perfect place for your Jersey cows to cool off. Let's go take a look."

As they tramped across the field, Ellie surveyed the sunny plot. With plenty of wide-open fields and a few shaded, woodsy areas, it was the kind of place she'd always imagined building a home, a real home, someday. Not that her bank account would let her seriously consider it. Most months, she played bill bingo hoping to get everything paid on time.

Her thought flicked to her conversation with Lou Ellen. As much as Lou Ellen bemoaned her single status, she got asked out a lot, an incredible feat for their insular community. Her unreasonable pickiness was what kept her single. Ellie couldn't remember the last time someone had asked her out. Most of the people she was around told her she reminded them of their daughter… or granddaughter.

Still, her singleness was a problem for another day. Now, she needed to focus. If she could make a quick sale on this lot, she might actually be able to pay to fix her stove before it blew her shack of a house up. A flash of red grabbed her attention as they entered the trees surrounding the pond.

"Hold up!" Her client obligingly halted behind her. She pulled her phone out and zoomed in as much as her shaking hand would allow. Squinting at the picture, she smiled. It had turned out clear. And in the center was a red-bellied woodpecker.

"That's a pretty picture." The man smiled at her.

"I'm an amateur bird-watcher. Been trying to spot one of these for ages."

He nodded, "My wife likes to watch the birds out at her feeders too. Last year, it was all about the hummingbirds. This year, I put up Martin houses for her."

"Oh! I'd love to do that. I just don't have the poles." Ellie led him to the pond, and he stood gazing at the water.

"This spot is lovely." He grinned at her. "And perfect for my Jersey girls." He held out his hand. "Tell you what, I've got some extra poles. You get me a good deal on this passel, and I'll drop off a set of Martin houses for you."

She shook his hand. "Now that's a deal I'll take."

Chapter 3

Grant straightened his tie and tugged down his cuffs as he watched the council members file out of the conference room. Bo patted him conciliatorily on the shoulder while Herb and Betty just hustled past while refusing to make eye contact. All three had unanimously voted down his proposal. Again.

"Grant. Would you come in here?" Mayor Patty called from her office down the hall. He kicked at the carpet then went to face his judgment.

Grant sat. In silence, Mayor Patty flipped through his proposal, turning each page with a slowly theatrical wave of her hand, her ebony skin gleaming in the afternoon light. Her left eyebrow lifted as she turned the last page and leaned back in her chair. Tugging at his collar, Grant forced himself not to glance at the clock ticking loudly on the wall.

She closed the binder on her polished desk with a sigh and steepled her fingers, her bangle bracelets tinkling as they settled into place on her forearms. "I have to say, I'm disappointed."

Grant's shoulders sank beneath the weight he'd been trying to ignore for weeks. He didn't know what else to do for this town. No one would talk to him much less share their ideas…

Mayor Patty's voice cut into his racing thoughts. "Honestly, I can see the work you've put into the background research. It's incredibly detailed." Her fingers flipped through the pages quickly. "But your ideas for future development—they're just not what we need right now."

She *hmmed* in her throat. "It seems like stuff and nonsense, to me. Murals? Some facade clean-up. A little razzle-dazzle on the internet. Infrastructure improvements we've tried for years to get funding for. I simply don't see how this will get people excited." She dropped her hands, thumbs drumming on the cover. "I need more. Something tangible. A way to get people buzzing."

Buzzing. He nodded, even as his fists clenched in his lap. Crossing his legs, he leaned forward. "Do you have any ideas? About things that might get people excited?"

Leveling a kind look at him, she gestured out the window. "The bar is pretty low. Most would just like to have the potholes fixed. Full-time jobs."

They had been over all of this before. Grant let out a breath and inclined his head. "I understand. But this plan is long-term. If we can improve Midnight Bluff's image, we can attract more businesses to move here. Get those jobs. Our company will help you with the infrastructure grants." He held his palms up. "A lot can be accomplished with a little bit of manpower even if the funds are lacking. We just need people to believe."

Shuffling the papers to the side, Mayor Patty stood and walked to the door, forcing him to stand and follow. "And

Chapter 3

I believe there are better ways to spark enthusiasm. But I'll give you a bit of time to prove me wrong. Two weeks. If you don't have any community buy-in on your plan by then, scrap it and find me something new." She patted his arm. "You're a smart man, and your boss speaks highly of you. I have every confidence. I want an update on your progress Friday." With a wave, she shut her frosted glass door in his face.

* * *

"Grant, we've already wasted too much time and too many resources on this town. I've propped you up on this as long as I can." Todd slurped his coffee, loud and obnoxious, in Grant's ear. "We need results by the end of April, or we have to pull the plug on this project." He took another loud sip, and Grant snatched the phone away from his ear. "You know how that will look to the board after Vermont."

Anxiety bloomed in his chest, tarry and clinging. "I'll get the buy-in. I just have to find the right angle." Grant stared up at the clouds overhead, dingy with rain. He tugged at his collar again. Even when on an overcast day in March, it was warm and humid in Mississippi. "Look, this town is a great opportunity for revitalization. I need a little more time is all."

"And you have it, man. I believe in you. You *used* to do good work." The implication was clear, and Grant winced at the undertone of displeasure. "Just find me that angle now." The line clicked, and Grant stared at his blinking screen, frustrated, as the first few drops of rain struck down. Todd hadn't offered any helpful advice, instead zeroing in the town council's rejection of yet another proposal.

Looking around the misty square, Grant spotted the softly glowing "Open" light at Loveless Bakery and dashed for it. As he bolted through the door with a jangle of bells, he groaned at the effort he'd wasted. He was soaked to the bone, the mist having turned to a downpour in the blink of an eye. He tossed his briefcase on a gingham-covered table and ran his hands over his face and through his hair, squeegeeing the water off.

Glancing out the window, he studied the clouds overhead, wondering how long until it was sunny again. Knowing his luck, this downpour would only last a couple of minutes but leave him damp for hours.

Squinting through the window down Main Street, Midnight Bluff looked almost charming with the lights of Southern Comfort Bar and the bingo hall blinking in the distance. Even the derelict cinema held a shade of its former glory through the forgiving curtains of rain. Nearby sat a grey truck, a quirky and faded logo reading "Mr. Fixit: A/C, Plumbing, No Electric" on the side.

"You look like a drowned rat." Willow, the owner of the bakery, stood behind the counter, one hand on her hip, the other resting atop the glass case, and a wry smile on her lips. "And you're getting my floors all wet."

"I'm standing on the mat," he muttered as he shook his hands out, flinging drops everywhere.

"Just—stand there. I'll get you something to dry off with." She disappeared into the back with a swish. As Grant waited, he slid his soggy jacket off and held it awkwardly to the side, making sure it dripped on the mat and not the slick floor.

As she reappeared, he apologized. "Sorry about this. I wasn't expecting rain."

"It's no problem, sugar." She gave him a handful of clean

Chapter 3

dishtowels and took his coat, opening the door and wringing it out onto the pavement outside. "You know what they say about the weather in Mississippi. If you don't like it, wait five minutes."

He looked at her, bemused. "I've never heard that before." Chuckling, he stepped gingerly across the floor in his slick-bottomed dress shoes while he patted at his face and neck. "It's catchy though. Very homespun."

Willow shrugged as she hung up his coat on a rack by the door. "That's us. Homespun." She strolled back behind the counter. "Your usual?"

"Let's do one of the chocolate croissants with it this time."

She eyed him. "The meeting went that bad, huh?"

Dang, this girl was observant. Slowly, he nodded. But Willow was down-to-earth, and she didn't force her advice on anyone unless you asked for it. Which was one of the things Grant appreciated about her. Besides the perfect pastries and her willingness to talk to him.

"Mayor Patty wasn't as excited about my plan as I hoped she'd be."

Willow handed him the croissant on a small plate and a cup of coffee; she raised her eyebrows, inviting him to continue.

He returned to the table with his briefcase. "Actually, she didn't like it at all. 'Stuff and nonsense,' I believe were her exact words." The description stung.

Willow grimaced as she wiped down the counter. "What are you going to do?"

"I have no freaking clue. I'm supposed to be getting the community involved or new ideas or something." He pulled off a piece of the flaky pastry and bit into it, savoring the flaky bread as it melted over his tongue. "But you and Patty are about the only ones who will talk to me in this town anymore." He took another bite, then blew on his coffee.

Willow frowned as she loaded a tray of cookies into the glass case. "No one? You haven't tried Herb over at the hardware store? Or Vada?"

"Avoid me like the plague." Grant waved a hand. "Herb's on the council—he thought my 1% sales tax idea to support the infrastructure was loony. Told me today in the council meeting it would drive what little business Midnight Bluff does have right on out of here. And Vada hates my guts for all the obvious reasons…" He trailed off, staring out the window into the rain. He couldn't blame her after the stunts he'd pulled with Cress.

"I wouldn't say hate." Willow smiled at him, mischief in her eyes. "Strongly dislike, maybe. But she'd still help you if you asked. That's what we do around here. Just because someone disagrees with your idea doesn't mean they hate you as a person."

Grant shook his head. That had not been his experience. Sure, people gave him directions or would help him carry heavy things to his car. But they didn't linger for conversation with him like they did with their neighbors. And Lou Ellen the other day made it very clear why. He brushed at his now-smooth face. At least he didn't look like a hobo anymore. Still, he was an outsider around here and that wasn't going to change.

"Oh, come on! We're not that bad." Willow set her tray and came around the end of the counter to lean against the front of the register. "Everyone is friendly enough."

"To you, the supplier of sugary treats." He smiled as he took another bite of his croissant, and Willow chuckled.

Chapter 3

"You got me there. But you have to understand, I'm not from around here either." He looked at her a little more closely. She held up her hands. "Shocking, I know. But I've only been here a couple of years. I know what it's like to be an outsider, too."

He narrowed his eyes as he considered her. "So, what did you do?"

She grinned and held out a foot for his inspection. She had on a pair of well-worn cowboy boots. "Took off my heels and bought myself a pair of boots. Figured out how to drink beer without gagging."

He made a face. "Heels aren't really my style."

Willow threw her head back, laughing. "C'mon. You know what I mean!"

He thought for a minute. "The beer doesn't sound so bad."

"There you go!" A timer went off in the back and she turned to see about it. "Think of a couple ways you can let your hair down and relax and you'll have people talking to you in no time."

As she disappeared, he bit into the buttery croissant, missing Madison, Wisconsin—even his sad little cubicle at Renewzit—and wondering if he'd ever find a place around here that did great sushi. But he supposed he could settle for a pair of jeans, a cold beer, and someone, finally, talking to him about anything other than budget projections and tax incentives.

Chapter 4

"Hey, Will!" Ellie called as she clattered into the bakery. "Will!" It took a second for the man at the table next to the door with crumbs all over his face who was staring at her to register as Grant, the poor sap from Cress' wedding and receiver of Lou Ellen's wrath.

Ellie pulled the hood of her raincoat back and smiled. "Oh, hey! You're…" she held out a hand and took a step forward. As her foot hit the shiny floor, she knew she'd made a mistake changing out of her mucky boots and wearing her flip-flops into the shop. Her foot flew out from under her, sliding her down into an awkward half-split as she grabbed for anything to stop her fall.

Which turned out to be Grant's leg. Or in this case, nearly his crotch as her hand collided with his hip. Even as her eyes watered from her knee slamming into the floor, she began stammering apologies and scrambling to rise.

"Oh, my God! I… I am so…"

A massive hand wrapped around her forearm, stopping her

Chapter 4

babbling, and gently lifted her to her feet as if she weighed no more than a kitten. The heady scent of orange blossoms washed over her as the warm hand steadied her. Dazed, she looked up into stunning hazel eyes.

"Are you alright?" Grant frowned down at her.

Ellie licked her lips and nodded, not trusting herself to form coherent words. He pointed at her leg. "Is your knee…?"

A throbbing enveloped her leg and she looked down to see blood soaking through her jeans. "Oooowww!" Hobbling to a chair, she plopped down, her backpack hanging awkwardly from her shoulder, and winced as she peeled the torn fabric away from the wound. Grant hovered over her.

Willow appeared in the doorway to the back. "What's all the ruckus?" Her eyes widened as she took in the scene. She flitted away and returned in mere seconds with a first-aid kit.

Grant took it from her. "Let me." He knelt in front of Ellie, and she shivered as his long, gentle fingers brushed across her knee, wiping away the blood with a gauze pad. Willow hovered at his shoulder.

"Oh, you don't have to!"

Glancing up at her from beneath the fringe of his lashes, he winced sympathetically. She sucked in her breath at his intense gaze, his hazel eyes shifting shades mesmerizingly in the stormy light from the window. "It's kinda my fault. I'd like to make it right." With a chuckle, he added, "I'm Grant Emberson, by the way."

"I know." She stuttered at his confused look, her heart inexplicably racing. She tried to explain, "Or I know of you. You're the one helping Mayor Patty."

He nodded. "That's me." A wrinkle appeared between his eyebrows, and Ellie resisted the urge to smooth it with her thumb.

Willow piped up, "Oh, Grant! *This* is Ellie Winters." Ellie looked up at Willow, bewildered by the sudden excitement in her voice.

"Yeah, Will?" Whatever had gotten into her friend, it had her unreasonably excited.

"No, what I mean is. You're Ellie!" Willow repeated herself with a flourish of her hand as if it meant something significant.

Grant turned and stared at her, mouth open and brow wrinkled. Rolling her eyes, Willow explained to him, "You know? That thing we were just talking about. Getting people to talk to you?"

He turned back to Ellie and pulled a Band-Aid out of the kit. "Way to make me sound like a total loser, Willow."

Willow punched his shoulder—his very muscled shoulder, Ellie noted—and he shot Willow a glare. "Hey! You're the one who was whining about it, not me." Ellie watched this exchange, gripping the edges of her chair. What did this have to do with her? Willow gestured at Ellie again. "Ellie's the only real estate agent…"

"Broker," Ellie corrected.

"…broker," Willow continued unphased, "In the area. She knows everybody!"

Ellie shrugged as Grant carefully placed a second Band-Aid over her already purpling knee. "It's true. But what does that have to do with anything?"

Grant opened his mouth, but Willow cut him off. "Oh, Mayor Patty hated his plan to revamp the town."

Ellie tried not to smile. Could have seen that one coming from a mile away. An outsider tell them what they needed? She looked at Grant, trying to keep a straight face. "What did

Chapter 4

she not like?"

"Everything," Willow answered again. Ellie stared at Willow pointedly. She made a little zipping motion across her mouth and went back to the counter.

"What did she not like?" she asked Grant again as they stood, Grant towering over her. He shoved his hands in his pockets and stared at the floor.

"Pretty much what Willow said: everything." He looked at her and tilted his head. "I have to get some community buy-in or go back to the drawing board."

"Huh." Ellie tapped her chin. She had a lot of properties all over the county to move; she didn't have the time to get involved with side projects right now. As she was about to politely demure and say that was tough luck, she saw his broad shoulders sag.

"It's such a shame. This place has so much potential; I just wish people could imagine it like I can. I guess that's what I was trying to do with my plan. Give them a glimpse of what the future could be like here."

A spark lit up inside of her. This town had given her so much, had taken her in when she would have gone to an orphanage far away. With a rush, she realized that a complete outsider had seen something she'd known about her home all along. Plus, more business would mean more real estate sales. And she was nothing if not practical.

"I'd love to help," she said. Grant blinked as she dug her wallet out of her backpack. "Here's my card. If there's anything I can do, just give me a call." She shook her damp hair back. "Like Willow said, I know everybody, so I can make introductions if you need them."

He studied the card for a second then slipped it into his own wallet. "Thank you. I'll keep it in mind." She knew a brush-off anywhere, and her elation sank.

He smiled as he held out his hand. "It was nice to meet you, Ellie. I'll see you around?"

Forcing a smile in return, she shook. "Sure! See you."

As he strode out the door, she couldn't help admiring how tall and well-muscled his back was even through his dampened suit. Or maybe because of it. With a little shake, she turned to Willow. "What are the odds he will give me a call?"

Willow tilted her head. "I'd say between zilch and not likely."

Ellie looked out the door again at Grant's back retreating through the downpour. "Still, he seemed nice enough. I don't see why people talk about him like he's some bogeyman. What do you think?"

"Of Grant?" Willow blinked at her. "Oh, he's a bit full of himself. Overly serious about his job. But I'd say, nice enough."

Ellie hitched her purse farther up her shoulder. "Can't fault him for being serious about his job."

Sticking out her tongue, Willow pulled open a drawer. "Speaking of workaholics, Vada was in earlier this morning. She said Mr. Stevens dropped by the Co-Op."

"Mr. Stevens!" She leaned over the counter. "Why didn't she call me? I would have been here in two seconds!"

"Girl, cool your jets. We got you covered. She got his number and—get this—he was talking about wanting to sell the old catfish plant."

"You can't be serious! That's huge."

Willow nodded, grinning. She handed Ellie a piece of yellow-lined notebook paper which she tucked into her purse after memorizing the number.

"Oh, this could make my year." Ellie's mind spun. If she could

Chapter 4

get the plant sold... She might be able to replace her roof. Even pay off her mortgage. At the very least, she wouldn't have to worry about paying the gas bill.

She reached over the counter and hugged Willow. "Thank you. You have no idea what this means to me!"

Patting her back, Willow laughed. "Hey! We're all family here. We look after one another." Ellie's heart swelled. She was so glad that was true in Midnight Bluff.

Another jingle of the bells announced the arrival of a breathless Dottie. Shedding her clear plastic poncho in a whirl of droplets that sent Willow scurrying for a mop, Dottie swept over to Ellie.

"Hey, doll! Just the lady I've been hoping to see. What do you know about Airbnb?"

Before Ellie could explain that she wasn't in the short-term rental business, Dottie launched into her spiel, her heart-shaped face lighting up. "Ever since Ronnie left..."

Ellie echoed dutifully, "That rat."

"I've been racking my brains on what to do with myself, and you know I've rented out the rest of the farm to Floyd Kelly for timber farming, but I've got all those silos and barns and the old sharecropper shacks that Ronnie insisted on keeping up. And I saw just *the cutest* idea on Pinterest—"

Holding up a hand to stem the flood of words, Ellie asked, "Dottie, I do have an appointment in a few minutes." It was sort of true. She had an appointment with her lunch, which was already several hours late. "Can you skip to your point, please?"

"Course, doll. I was thinking of fixing the places up real nice and Airb-n-b-ing..." Dottie bounced a finger on the awkward syllables. "...them out. And I was hoping you could guide me through that process? You're our resident expert!"

Inhaling through her nose, Ellie tried not to let her consternation show. "Let me think on it." Willow was staring at them, eyes wide. "Rentals aren't my area of..." She waved a hand. "... expertise. But I'll see if it's something that might make sense for this market."

Dottie bobbled her head. And Ellie braced herself for what she was about to say. "But Dottie, have you thought this through? How many renters would you really get out here in Midnight Bluff?" Some of the light left her eyes, and Ellie kicked herself for cratering a possible payday. "I'm not saying it's a terrible idea. I just don't want to set you up for failure."

"I was just thinking with the farm and the goats and chickens and cows and vegetable garden and all..." Pressing her lips together, Dottie shook her head. "Well, it sounds so silly to say it now. But I was thinking I would set it up like one of those experiences you see on TV. City folk could come unplug for a few days. Experience country life. I could teach them a bit about homesteading."

It was such a wonderful dream. But Ellie just couldn't imagine someone with suede shoes and a fancy manicure wanting to come chase chickens. Then again, maybe she was wrong.

She touched Dottie's arm. "I'll look into it. I promise." Dottie's face lit up. Just one more thing on her ever-growing to-do list.

Chapter 5

Mr. Pearce, the Municipal Clerk, narrowed his eyes at Grant while his bony fingers tapped the counter. Already sensing this wasn't going to be a quick visit, Grant set his briefcase on the yellowed floor next to his feet and leaned his elbows on the counter. Coughing against the ancient scrim of mildew and cigarette smoke lingering in the air, he pulled the address he needed from his pocket.

"I need to look up who owns this parcel of land." Grant slid the creased paper across the scuffed and ink-stained counter to Mr. Pearce. With a sniff, Mr. Pearce flipped the paper open with the tip of his pencil. His eyebrows shot up.

"Afraid I can't help you." He tapped the paper closed with the eraser and slid it back across, already turning to disappear into the rows of filing cabinets.

"Wait! I just need to know who owns the property so I can speak with them—"

Mr. Pearce whirled around, papers along the counter fluttering. "Son, you listen to me. You've been speaking with just about half the dang county, including my daughter. Been getting people mighty riled up over a good deal o' nothing. I suggest you quit sticking your nose where it don't belong."

The pale light from the fluorescent caught the irises of Mr. Pearce's eyes, making them flash. Grant took in the man's thinning comb-over and sunken eyes. Only his striking nose and the flush creeping up his neck bore any resemblance to Lou Ellen.

Remembering Lou Ellen's mortified face, Grant tried to apologize. "I'm sorry that I startled Lou Ellen the other day. I just…"

"You just nothing." He cut Grant off. Clenching his jaw, Grant fought against the heat licking up his chest at this rudeness. He would gladly apologize, but he would not stand being humiliated again. Mr. Pearce continued his diatribe. "All you big city boys just waltz in here thinking you can upset things and it don't matter, well I'll tell you right now—"

"Mr. Pearce." Grant's voice cut in, sharp and flat. He pressed a hand against the counter. How did that real estate lady—Ellie—deal with these difficult people? "I have a job to do, as do you. This is an office of *public* records, of which I am legally within my rights to request." He took a breath and pushed the paper back across. "Now, if you please, the owner of this property."

Snatching the paper, Mr. Pearce poked at a few keys on an ancient computer. "All right, but you'll see. The doctor ain't going to want to speak to you either."

Through his teeth, Grant muttered, "I'm sure," as Mr. Pearce scribbled a name and phone number on the sheet and shoved it back to him. Moving as decorously as he could, Grant slid the page into his briefcase, nodded to the glaring clerk, and

Chapter 5

hastened out of the musty office and into the blazing sun.

* * *

With a yank, Grant took off his tie then jerked open the top three buttons of his shirt. He'd been sitting all afternoon on the only shaded bench in Midnight Bluff's square making phone calls to Dr. Clay Washburn. The man's cell phone didn't have voicemail set up—odd for a heart doctor—so Grant had tried his clinic in Cleveland only to be brusquely told by an overly zealous assistant with a pert voice that the doctor wouldn't speak with solicitors before he'd even gotten two words out.

She'd refused to let him leave a message.

The man had no presence online outside of his listing with the clinic, so Grant had been unable to find an email address. Groaning, he slouched against the bench and wondered if it was possible to turn into a puddle of goo. How did people stand this heat? And it was only March.

He wondered how that cute-as-a-button realtor managed in this heat. With her rolled-up sleeves and worn-in jeans, she looked like she was no stranger to dealing with the elements—weather or people.

Desperate, he shot a text to Dr. Washburn's cell. Maybe the man was a texter. Because a sixty-year-old doctor would text a stranger back. Heaving a sigh worthy of a sixteen-year-old, Grant stood, mopping sweat off his brow.

He knew he just had to keep moving. If he could succeed on one thing, he could use that momentum to accomplish more. That first success was always the hardest with these sorts of projects.

And if it involved getting out of this heat, all the better. His mind wandered again to the real estate agent he'd met earlier. All the real estate agents he knew were so tight-laced; but she'd seemed laidback, at ease. Was that how she dealt with showing property in these insane conditions: the mugginess, mosquitoes, and ridiculous pollen count? Just the thought of it made him swipe at his nose.

Trying to focus, he turned towards the center of town and cut directly across the square towards Herb's Hardware Store, not caring that he was jaywalking. There was barely any traffic anyway. The bells shop owners seem to favor instead of actual alarms rang out as he pushed open the door and paused just inside the threshold to let his eyes adjust.

Herb's deep voice rang out from the back. "Be right with you."

Grant dawdled by the door, gawking at a set of saw blades that looked fit for a horror movie before tentatively stepping further into the hardware store. There was something about the sawdust and motor oil smell of this place that always freaked him out.

With a slam, Herb stamped out of the backroom, making a tremendous amount of noise for such a small man. Barely coming up to Grant's shoulder, he did not doubt that the muscle-bound miniature of Hephaestus could easily take him in a fight. Especially considering Grant had never been in a real fight with anything more than a spreadsheet.

"Oh. Hey, Grant," Herb said much less energetically as he dumped an armload of hammers onto the counter. "Did that washer work for you?"

Blinking a few times, Grant remembered he'd come in a couple of weeks ago for a washer to fix his eternally dripping

Chapter 5

sink. At the time, he'd decided to handle it instead of the ordeal of Mr. Tisdale talking his ear off for an hour then rummaging around his apartment looking for other "maintenance issues."

The sink was still dripping. He'd forgotten he needed wrenches and screwdrivers and… things.

Remembering Ellie's bright face, he smiled at Herb, trying to remain upbeat. "Worked like a charm."

"Great. Great." Herb kept his eyes on the tools in front of him. "What can I do for you today?" He began sorting out the hammers, grouping them loosely by size.

Scratching at the back of his head, Grant looked around, not sure how to frame this request. "You own most of the properties in this part of town, right?"

Herb looked at him then as he ran his tongue over his teeth. His expression was cool and guarded, his eyes lidded. "Su-u-u-re. You looking to buy something or just curious?"

Grant was getting way too familiar with that expression. He leaned against the counter, trying to seem at ease even as a mallet landed too close for comfort by his elbow.

"The mayor and I are trying to spruce things up to get people excited about this revitalization plan. I was wondering if there was any way I could convince you to spiff up the place." He jerked his thumb toward the row of papered-over storefronts and rubble-strewn lots outside.

Working his lips back-and-forth, Herb thought for a moment, hands moving slowly as he sorted more hammers. Finally, he turned to Grant. "Look, I ain't got nothing against you." Grant's thoughts hopped skeptically to their yelling match a couple of months ago. "You seem like a decent guy, even if you're a bit of an odd duck. But the last time the mayor roped me into some scheme like this, nothing much came of it except Willow's bakery… and that crazy ex of hers who skipped town and left a bunch of junk behind in my best space." He scooped up an armful of tools and headed towards a shelf, Grant trailing him.

"And, as much as I like Willow, I'm not eager to lose out on rent again." He began tossing the hammers onto racks with ear-splitting clangs.

Rubbing one hand into another, Grant tried again. "I completely understand your hesitancy. But this wouldn't be supplemental rent. What we were thinking is cleaning up the storefronts. Clearing out any trash or debris. Fixing broken windows. Touching up paint. Making things look attractive to potential renters." Herb was already shaking his head.

"All that 'potential' *sounds* great. Really. It does." Herb hung up one last hammer and turned around, hands on hips. "But it's a lot of labor and materials for a lot of maybes. Just like always. And the town wouldn't be putting anything in. *You* wouldn't be putting anything in."

He looked Grant up and down, taking in his sweat-drenched dress shirt and scuffed Oxford shoes with quirked brows. "Look, I started buying up all this property the first time Patty hatched a crazy idea to get this place back on its feet. Thought it would really be something." He pointed at his own face. "And I've got jack to show for it except a crazy property tax bill and one tenant who just started paying this year. I know as well as you do that you can't guarantee it will go anywhere." He shook his head. "So, sorry, can't help ya."

"Is there anything I can do to change your mind?" Grant stood, hands shoved in his pockets. His fingers clenched around his silent cell phone.

Shaking his head, Herb strode past him. "Don't think so,

Chapter 5

buddy." He glanced over his shoulder. "You're welcome to tackle it yourself if you care so much, but I won't be doing it."

Running his hands through his hair, Grant hefted his briefcase then gave him a half-hearted wave. "Well, thanks for your time." He turned on his heel and pushed open the door. As he stepped out into the scorching sun, he glanced over his shoulder to see Herb watching, arms crossed over his stomach as he leaned against the counter.

He trudged back to his bench and slouched onto it. He stared down at himself. Sweat ringed his armpits and neck. His shoes need a good polishing, scuffed as they'd gotten the last few days trudging back and forth talking to various townspeople. There was no way he could go back inside the courthouse to work at one of the conference tables looking like this. And he had absolutely nothing to show for it.

How did Ellie do it, showing properties and being so friendly to these stubborn people, day in and day out? He had no clue and he'd been here for months.

Muttering curses, he decided to call it quits for the day and head to the gym by his apartment in Cleveland. If he was going to sweat, he was at least going to get something for his misery.

He'd worry about what Mayor Patty would say about his lack of "buy-in" tomorrow.

* * *

Mayor Patty tapped her fingers against the pages of Grant's proposal. Today's jewelry theme was rings. Lots and lots of rings. They sparkled in the sunlight from the window and sent shards of light slashing across the room

She frowned at the paper. "So, your plan hinges on making the storefronts and square as attractive as possible?"

Grant nodded, pressing his knuckles into the sides of his legs. It was an oversimplification of a multi-stage process, but he just didn't have any fight left in him.

"And you want to paint a couple of splashy murals on… private property? Am I reading this correctly?"

"Yes." His voice rasped out, thin and cracked.

"Which you haven't even gotten permission to use?"

All he could do was nod again.

The mayor continued, her frown deepening. "And this is so that our citizens can *imagine* a bustling Main Street with occupied storefronts and lofts?"

He forced some saliva into his parched mouth. "Exactly."

"And yet, you've failed to get the cooperation of a single Main Street business owner to make this vision happen?" She tapped the papers into a tight bundle and laid them down in a neat pile as she stared at Grant.

Rubbing his sweaty palms on his trousers, he tried to explain, "There have been a few roadblocks convincing the owners to…"

"…to pitch into an idea that may never pay off without something more concrete to first prove the idea. How, exactly, do you plan to capture the traffic to make Main Street so bustling?" Grant's tongue clung to the roof of his mouth as all his answers fled away. He had ideas, but nothing he'd put to paper beyond the initial steps he'd so blithely thought he'd get approved.

The emeralds in her dangling earrings gleamed as she shook her head. "Grant, darling, I have to say I'm disappointed. Again."

Chapter 5

His throat tightened, and he leaned back in his chair. "I'll keep trying. These things take time—"

She held up a hand, cutting him off. "Sweetie, I know the people of this town. I've been through tornados, sewage backups, and the bottom of our water tower rusting out." Leaning forward, she rested on her elbows and nodded across the hall.

"I've birthed a baby on that conference table in there when the ambulance couldn't get here from Cleveland in time." Grant winced at the thought of how unsanitary that was, but she continued. "When push comes to shove, I get down in the dirt with them to get things done." Shaking her head, she continued, "If you haven't been able to convince them by now, it's because they simply don't trust you to be there for them. They've got to see you show up."

With a flick of her wrist, she handed the stack of pages back to him. "Denied." As he sputtered, she spoke firmly, her eyes soft at the corners, "You have a week to get me something more concrete—to impress me. Or I will let your boss know that we will not be continuing with this contract."

As he stood, scrambling for his briefcase, she called, "Grant?"

He turned to her, hives already beginning to break out beneath his shirt. "Good luck. I hope for both of our sakes that you come up with a wonderful plan." The corners of her lips forced themselves into a smile that didn't match the deep crease between her eyebrows. As he fumbled out the door, she was already reaching for the phone.

Somehow, he made it outside and to the parking lot. Slamming his car door behind him, Grant rested his head back, breathing in through his nose and out through his mouth before he cranked the engine and took off down Main Street.

He was so antsy his fingers were tingling and he felt a migraine coming on. Massaging his temple, he narrowly avoided a pothole that would have eaten his tire as he bumped down the road.

On the outskirts of Midnight Bluff, he halted, staring down the road through a flush of woods at the abandoned catfish plant in the distance. A tiny real estate sign tilted in front of it, unreadable from this distance. Sunlight poured over the rusted red roof and dripped down the corrugated sides. The windows looked mostly intact, and except for the dilapidated chain-link fence surrounding it and the rust, the building looked to be in decent shape. He rubbed at his mouth then dug for his wallet.

As he pulled her card out and began punching her number into his phone, his mind spun. There were buildings like this all over the area. And Ellie had said she knew everybody. He wondered if she just might be his ticket to talking the business owners into…

His hand dropped. She couldn't solve the problem that Mayor Patty had officially rejected his proposal. And he had no clue what to do about it. What would even appeal to yokels out in the middle of nowhere? He slumped against the wheel, fighting the rising panic.

If he didn't get this contract executed, he would lose his job. Todd had made that clear. Sucking in a deep breath, he hit the call button.

One problem at a time. Right now, he just needed a way in with the locals. And Ellie might be his last shot.

Chapter 6

Sorry. The word hung hollow as Ellie slid the phone into her pocket and swung back up into the saddle. That was the third call this week. Since listing the plant for Mr. Stevens, she'd gotten plenty of interest.

Marketing had always been her strong suit. Having some sweet photography skills helped when it came to being a real estate agent. She could make the most gutted-out dump look like an artsy, airy space. A briar patch became a great looking field just ready for planting.

But the people calling for the catfish plant? Whole different ball game. She bet that Grant didn't have to deal with this kind of thing with his fancy clients in Minnesota or Seattle or wherever he was from. Pulling her shirt down as she found the comfiest spot in the saddle, she shook herself to clear her head of his swoon-worthy shoulders.

As she settled her feet into the stirrups, Vada looked at her curiously. "Another client?"

Shaking her head, Ellie eased her big grey horse, General,

out of the paddock before Vada could guess that her thoughts had been anywhere but work. They headed for the edge of the woods. "'Nother bust. That plant is kicking my butt. I keep getting nibbles on it, but not a good bite."

"Huh." Vada stayed silent as she navigated her sorrel horse, Flick, around a fallen log as they worked their way deeper down the trail. As she let General navigate his way through a swollen stream, Ellie held onto her pommel, breathing against the sudden cold of the water flooding over her boots.

"What do you think is keeping buyers from following through?" Vada's question floated over Ellie's shoulder as she swayed up the bank and into a clearing flooded with daffodils. The clop of Flick's hooves came to a stop beside her as they surveyed the glowing scene.

"I always forget just how beautiful it is around here until I get back out into the woods." Ellie patted General's neck.

Vada cut her eyes toward her. "This is why I'm always on you to come riding with me." She tugged on Flick's reins, easing them around the edge of the glade. "You gotta be out in nature if you want to stay in touch with your roots."

"And it has nothing to do with you needing help exercising the horses!" Ellie called after her.

With a laugh, Vada just waved at her. "We need to do a girl's camping trip soon. Me, you, and Willow. Maybe do a little fishing on the bayou."

Nodding happily, Ellie swayed along on General enjoying the fresh air on her face. Did Grant like horseback riding? She'd never seen him in anything more casual than jeans and a button-up.

"Earth to Ellie! You still never answered my question. Why ain't anybody buying the plant?"

Chapter 6

Grant's hazel eyes flashed before her. She had not been able to get him off her mind and it was beginning to annoy her. She tried to concentrate on the trail. "Well... it's only been on the market for a couple of weeks." She was hedging her answer and she knew it.

"Girl! I've seen you sell things the next day. Don't give me that!" Chuckling, Ellie worked the reins nervously in her fingers then released them at General's outraged head toss.

"Mr. Stevens... wants to sell it intact."

As they passed back into the shade, she watched Vada's back. Her shoulders tightened. "Intact? As in everything inside it too, intact?" Confusion laced her words, making them flutter with the new leaves brushing their cheeks.

Tension seeped out of Ellie that she wasn't the only one confused by her client's request. "Uh-huh. He wants to sell the whole thing in one go." She squeezed her knees as General hopped over a log. "He doesn't want to deal with selling off scrap to one buyer, bricks to another, and the land to a third." A spiderweb slapped her across the face, and she impatiently brushed it away. "I tried to explain that it would take much longer to sell this way... that it might be impossible with the equipment still inside. But he insisted."

She frowned as she thought of his words. *Miracle worker.* Like she could take a rusted hunk of metal and make it into a functioning building just anyone would want. And she'd been so excited for this property; now it was going to ruin her track record. Shaking her head, she glanced at Vada as the trail widened.

"Well, we'll just have to believe the right buyer will come along." Vada reached over and patted her arm awkwardly. "Surely it will appeal to someone."

"Surely," Ellie murmured. Her friend was trying to cheer her up. She didn't want to ruin their ride with her problems. With a flip of her ponytail, she smiled deviously at Vada. "So, did you hear the youth pastor up and quit?"

"What? No!" Vada's mouth formed a little O as she looked at Ellie. "How have I not heard about this?"

"I swear! I heard it from Lou Ellen. You know she works in the church office."

Vada sniffed and swiped a strand of hair back over her shoulder. "I suppose she'd know. Being up in everyone's business."

"Come on. You're just still holding a grudge about Lorene."

"A grudge is mild compared to..."

Ellie's phone rang, the notes to the Lilo & Stitch theme song ringing through the woods. General flicked his ears back in irritation. Snickering, Vada waved at her face. "I can't believe that is still your theme song!"

"Ohana means family!" Ellie chirped at Vada as she hit Answer with a grin.

"Ohana means family? Is this Ellie Winters?" A man's gravelly voice crackled over the line. She glanced at the caller ID. Her eyebrows shot up as disbelief nearly knocked her off General.

"Oh, hi Grant." If fantasizing got her what she wanted, she should daydream more often. She stared at Vada open-mouthed. After the way he'd brushed her off the other day, she had not been expecting him to call. "Yep, this is me. What can I do you for?" She cringed as the words stuttered out of her mouth. So smooth.

Vada halted Flick and reached for General's reins to bring him to a standstill as well. "Grant?" she mouthed at Ellie, eyes

Chapter 6

wide. She'd already heard Vada's opinion of Grant—at length. And it was not the shiny little daydream that Ellie had just been indulging in.

"Ummm... Look, I hate to call you like this. But I could use some local expertise on this project after all. I'd love to take you up on your offer. Are you available to meet?" His voice wavered, and she wasn't sure if it was the bad connection or nerves.

"Ok. Sure. I could do one meeting." Ellie paused, not sure what exactly he wanted to meet about. She supposed they could start with the basics: go over what he already had in the project, highlight areas for improvement, possibly put together an interest survey. "When do you want to get together?" Again, with the awkward phrasing. Vada pressed her lips together and squinched her eyes as she stared back at her.

Grant chuckled. "Would now work? The sooner the better, honestly." Brushing a sweaty chunk of hair back from her forehead, she looked around at the woods. "Now? Umm... I'm going to need a few minutes to get cleaned up and back to town." She rolled her eyes to the sky, promising herself to start working on setting boundaries. Tomorrow. She'd start tomorrow. "Does the bakery work?"

"Perfect. See you in a few." The line clicked. Ellie looked at her phone, stunned at the turn of events. Vada was laughing so hard, she bent over Flick's neck.

"Come on," she said as she straightened up and swiped at her face. "Let's get you back so you can get cleaned up for your date with Cress' ex."

"It's not a date!" Ellie screeched, startling a rabbit from a bush and making General dance to the side. As she struggled to calm General, she added, "It's a work meeting. I'm just doing him a favor. Really, I'm doing Mayor Patty a favor, if you think about it."

Her mind skittered to his hands on her knee, how pleasantly warm they had been—

"Mmhmm. You just keep telling yourself that." Vada peeked over her shoulder as she urged Flick back down the trail. "You're grinning like the Cheshire Cat."

Ellie wiped the smirk from her face. "I am not!" She began worrying at the reins again. "Is Cress going to be upset?"

"Girl! Cress ain't got a jealous bone in her body. And she just got married. He's fair game, if you go in for huge, hunky jerks." Vada shot her a conspiratorial look. "Besides, it's just a work meeting, right?" She stuck out her tongue and urged Flick into a trot, forcing Ellie to click at General to keep up. Barking out a laugh, she raced after her friend back to the barn, wind streaming through her hair and leaves slapping at her knees as she reveled in the warm spring day.

Chapter 7

From his table inside the Loveless Bakery, Grant looked at his watch and then out at the glare of the sun on the bricks of Main Street. Where was this woman? She'd said she be here in a few minutes. That was forty-five minutes ago.

Behind him, Willow chuckled. "Seriously, you have got to relax." She wiped down the counter for the third time. "Out here, a few minutes can mean a couple of hours."

He groaned. "I don't have all day."

She stared at him as she drug the damp cloth over the counter. "Don't you?"

Point taken. He turned back to his cup of coffee and hunched his shoulders. With no clue what to do with his proposal and no one willing to talk to him, he was back at square one. Scratch that: square zero.

He'd never floundered this much on a project, not even in Vermont. And he'd still managed to pull that one out at the last second. At least there was some industry to make use of in

Vermont. Unlike in Mississippi where there were just endless rows of corn and cotton and then… nothing.

With a sigh, he went back to staring out the window over his cooling cup of coffee. Finally, a windshield gleamed in the distance, and he shot to his feet and hustled outside.

"Dude, you have no chill!" Willow called after him as the bells clanged above the closing door. Not caring, he stood impatiently on the front walk as Ellie got out of her beat-up truck. She looked at him, blue eyes wide. His eyes swept over her curves, struck by the pleasing sweeps and tucks of her petite frame. Realizing he was staring at her, he snapped his eyes back to her face. Fortunately, she was preoccupied with scooping various notepads and pens into a scarred-up backpack.

"I get a welcoming committee?" The corners of her lips twitched upwards as she hefted the backpack onto her shoulder. He eyed its duct-taped straps with concern as he stepped forward.

"Can I get anything else for you?" He stepped forward and studied the inside of her truck, littered with binoculars, coffee cups, and notepads.

She shook her head as she ducked her eyes, crossing her arms over her chest. He chuckled, feeling his chest tighten as her damp braid swished over her shoulder. "All right then." As he eased her door closed, he waved towards the bakery, trying to be hospitable. He did have some manners, despite what everyone around here seemed to think of him. "After you."

Willow was already at his table, freshening his cup and pouring another for Ellie. She hugged Ellie as she settled in across from all his papers. "Good to see you, sweetie." Waving a finger at the table, she asked, "Need anything else before y'all

Chapter 7

get started?" At a shake of his head, she slid away behind the counter, obviously eavesdropping.

Grant watched as Ellie tucked a strand of hair that had fallen from her braid behind her ear and shook her head bemusedly. She chunked her backpack on the floor and leaned forward onto her elbows, peering at the papers. He slid into his chair and handed her a fresh copy of the proposal.

Clearing his voice, he began, feeling oddly nervous as her eyes scanned the sheets. "First, thank you for helping me." He clasped his hands, studying the worn denim of her shirt, light along the creases and frayed at the rolled-up cuffs. Her nails were chewed to the quick. At his stare, she shifted in her chair.

"Your notes are very thorough." Sitting the pages down, she picked up her cup of coffee. "So, did you need my help drafting the proposal for the mayor or..." He stared at her, confusion fuzzing his brain with white noise.

"Drafting?" The word dropped from his lips and splatted on the table. Her eyes widened and her fingers clenched around the cup. "No. No, this is the proposal right here." He tapped the papers in front of them.

Her brow knit and she coughed into her fist. Not coughed. Laughed. In consternation, he watched as she began pounding on her chest, laughing and sputtering on coffee so hard tears had begun to run down her face.

Huffing, he half-rose from his chair. "You don't have to help me if you don't want to!" Beginning to shuffle the papers into his briefcase, his mind was already spinning with how well and truly screwed he was. His last chance was sitting here, choking on coffee, laughing at him.

She reached across the table and grabbed his wrist, her fingers warm and dry. Eyes serious, she said, "Sit down, please.

I want to help. Really." Swiping at her face, she waved at the table. "I'm sorry. I shouldn't have laughed." She paused for a moment, tilting her head to the side. "Your... proposal... isn't bad. It just didn't include a lot of the things that I think matter to people around here. It seems very—"

"Shallow." Grant ground out the word. God, he was so tired of hearing that.

Ellie nodded quickly. "But not in a bad way!"

"How is shallow ever anything but bad?" He sat back in his chair with a grumble. This woman was so frustrating. Laughing at him one minute and agreeing with him backhandedly the next.

"People around here don't get the optics of things. How things need to look good to sell." She blew the loose strand of hair out of her face again then reached for her backpack. "Here. Let me show you." Pulling a camera out, she turned it on and flipped through some pictures. "Look at this place."

She handed him a shot of a house from directly in front of it that was clearly taken at high noon. Weedy flower beds, an old wire bed frame on the front porch, and askew shutters gave it a gaunt, haunted feel. "It's a dump. So?"

Without a word, she took the camera, clicked a button, and handed it back. "Now, what do you think?" Soft morning light washed over the same house. But the shutters now hung straight, the flower beds were cleaned out and covered in bright red pine straw, and a clean-swept porch gave it a fresh country feel.

He whistled. "I'd say it's got great bones and would be a good investment property."

Cress shook her head smiling. "That's exactly what the guy who bought it said two days after I listed it."

Chapter 7

Grant sat back and looked at her a little more closely. Freckles ran across the bridge of her nose and shadows rimmed her eyes. He guessed she didn't sleep very well. But something about her was fresh and appealing. Genuine. That was the word he was looking for.

Taking a deep breath, he gripped the edge of the table and admitted the truth. "Mayor Patty rejected my proposal. I have to scrap the whole thing because I can't get any community buy-in." He inhaled. "And my boss has given me a cut-off date as well. Things are… getting tight… for getting this done. I was hoping you could help me talk to some of the business owners. Get them on board with my ideas."

Ellie leaned over the papers, hand over her mouth, as she listened. "Scrap it? No. This is good." His heart flipped over in his chest. "We need to flesh it out. A lot. Zhuzh it up." With a glance at him, she raised an eyebrow. "Work on making you more approachable." She pulled a notepad from her backpack and began scribbling things in an unintelligible chicken scratch.

Grant glanced down at himself. "Approachable?"

"That suit is sharp as a knife. And people think you're going to cut them too."

He stared at her, mouth gaping open. At the counter, Willow snorted. "She's not wrong, man."

"What's wrong with being professional?"

Tapping his shoe where it lay across his opposite leg, Ellie smirked at him. "Knowing your audience. You can't talk to a blue-collar man when you look like a big-city fixer. It will be like trying to squeeze blood from a turnip."

What in the world… "But I am a big-city fixer! That's exactly what I've been hired to do."

Rolling her eyes, Ellie looked at him. "Look, I'm telling it to you straight. If you want people to listen to you, you got to look like you're going to listen to them. And they're going to assume by your clothes that you think you're better than them."

Grant crossed his arms. Of all the confounded things, his clothes were putting people off? He grumbled to himself. "If you say so. Just tell me what to do."

"All right. Jeans and a nice button-up are fine. Whatever shoes you have."

He snorted but didn't argue. Willow grinned at him from the counter, and he glared at her. She withdrew to the back, hands held up.

Muttering as she wrote, Ellie got to work on her notes. "Now on this plan, we could use a local heritage campaign." She drew what he thought was an arrow. "But that won't make sense without a Chamber of Commerce and…"

Static filled his mind as a hot poker ran through his chest. A Chamber of Commerce. He'd completely skipped one of the most important things any municipality needed. Wiping his hands over his face, he tilted back in his chair. What was wrong with him?

His lungs sizzled and seized with regret as he reached for the tissues in his pocket. "How did I miss that?" he wheezed.

Ellie glanced up. "To be fair, we don't even have a bank. And our post office runs from a closet in the courthouse. So…"

He shook his head, pressing the tissue to his nose. "That's not an excuse. A Chamber is so basic… It should have been the first thing—"

A gentle hand wrapping around his wrist shushed him. Ellie licked her lips as she leaned across the table staring intently at

Chapter 7

him. His arm tingled and warmed under her fingers. "Hey. I'm not about all that. Living in the past just drags you down. Keeps you from moving forward." She released his wrist. "Once we know better, we do better. Ok?"

He swallowed, finally able to take a deep breath for the first time in days. "Ok."

"Yaaaas, girl!" Willow clapped her hands. "Nail that speech!"

Blushing, Ellie giggled and propped her head on one hand, hiding her face. Utterly charmed, Grant smiled. Beauty, brains, and humility—that was a package he could work with.

His phone rang interrupting the moment. The caller ID said MOM. "Gotta take this. Be one sec." He'd been avoiding her calls all day and if he didn't answer soon, she was liable to send the National Guard after him. He wouldn't put it past her.

"Darling! I was starting to get worried about you!"

He rolled his eyes so hard to the ceiling he was pretty sure he strained something. "It's been less than forty-eight hours. You're not allowed to worry yet."

"I'm a mother. It's my God-given right to worry over my children all I want."

"I'm fine, Mom." Ellie glanced up at him, cheeks dimpling distractingly in amusement.

"You've been avoiding me. That's not fine. What's going on that you can't answer?"

"I'm busy." He looked over at Ellie and mouthed *sorry*. "Can I call you back? I'm with someone."

"I hope it's a girl. You've been so blue since Cress left you."

"It's not..." His eyes trailed to Ellie, scribbling away on her notepad. "Yes." A squeal nearly pierced his eardrum. "I'll call you later, all right? Love you. Bye." What had he just gotten himself into?

51

"Are you close with your parents?" Pinching the bridge of his nose, he wondered if Ellie was the type for big family Christmases, all the cousins crowded around the table, or more just her and her—he checked her ring finger—boyfriend?

She looked up at him, her expression curiously blank. "Nope." Shaking her head, she scribbled another note. "But family life is important here in Midnight Bluff, so I think focusing on family-friendly events and activities should be a big focus for us." Glancing at her watch, she began to pack up her stuff. "I've got a showing I've got to get to…"

Disappointed she had to leave so soon, he stood with her. His stomach knotted, thinking of using her sparse notes as a jumping-off point to rework his plan. Maybe he could pull it all together. Somehow. Her soft words cut through his spinning thoughts. "…But I can work with you some more tomorrow. If that's ok?"

Elation zinged through him. "Sure. I'll brainstorm some ideas tonight." He rubbed his hands together. Surely, he wasn't so blocked that he couldn't come up with… anything.

She patted his arm. "Why don't you check out Cleveland's website and walk around their downtown? They do some cool stuff that might inspire you."

He liked this woman, with all her ideas. Grinning now, he picked up her backpack for her. "That's perfect. My apartment is just off Sunflower Road."

Ellie gave a little hop. "I have an idea! Why don't I meet you at your place tomorrow, and we'll do a field trip through Cleveland, see the sites. I'll take you to the Chamber of Commerce. It'll be immersive. And you can see what a Delta city with a thriving downtown and active Chamber looks like."

"Works for me!" His heart sped up at the idea of having Ellie

Chapter 7

with him for a full day, getting to see Mississippi through the eyes of a local who adored this state. He gave her his address and they agreed to meet at eleven so most of the businesses would be fully open by then. As he watched her drive away, a lightness he hadn't felt in days filled him. Maybe, just maybe, they could tackle this project together.

Willow sauntered up beside him with a big grin. "So, you been living like a bachelor for the last six months, haven't you?"

Grant snatched his briefcase and sprinted out the door. "I've got to go clean!" Willow's laughter pealed after him.

Chapter 8

This couldn't be the address. Ellie looked at her phone then at the house then back at her phone to confirm she had the right number. Puzzled, she parked along the curb and got out, slowly sliding the straps of her backpack up onto her shoulders as she surveyed the beige ranch house with detached garage and workshop in front of her.

She hesitated on the front walk. Grant couldn't be renting the whole place, could he? There was a minivan sitting in the driveway; she was pretty sure he was driving a Prius. As she froze on the concrete, undecided, she heard the creak of a door and the thud of footsteps on stairs.

Grant's head popped around the corner of the house. At least he had listened to her and was dressed in jeans and a crisp Polo shirt instead of his suit. But he looked flustered, cheeks flushed and eyes wide with alarm. He waved her toward him. "Ellie!" His voice was low but urgent. "This way."

"Are you… all right?" She gripped the straps of her backpack tighter.

Chapter 8

"Yes, I just don't want to disturb my landlord." He waved at her again, arm circling faster. Haltingly, she followed him around the side of the house and up a flight of stairs above the garage.

And into a full loft apartment. She paused in the doorway and blinked against the suddenly dimmer light as she took it in. It was a bit spartan but neat and furnished with solid furniture. Not cheap IKEA crap.

"Oh." Laughing at herself, she leaned against the doorframe. "You had me worried for a second. But this is nice."

Grant brushed his hand against the back of a wooden chair at the tiny dining room table. It was more of a breakfast nook. They'd barely have room for both of them to pull their chairs out. She brushed her hair back as she considered the cramped quarters.

Maybe they could scooch the couch—

"Well, look at this!" The sudden voice behind her made her nearly jump out of her skin. A short man with a slight beer gut and the beginnings of a bald spot stood grinning behind her. "Grant didn't tell us he'd be having company." He stuck out his hand. "Mr. Tisdale, the landlord."

Ellie glanced at Grant who had rolled his eyes. The landlord must be a frequent rider on the busybody express. She looked back at Mr. Tisdale and his hand, still outstretched. Slowly, she shook his sweaty palm. "Hi, I'm Ellie."

"And how long will you be staying?" He looked over her shoulder at Grant pointedly. "We're grilling out tonight if you two want to join the family instead of staying in."

Crossing his arms, Grant stared back at him. "She's a colleague here for the afternoon for a work project."

Heat flared through Ellie's cheeks at the sudden implication.

"Yes! Just working. I live in Midnight Bluff... I'm in real estate so I..."

Mr. Tisdale waved his hands, grin still in place. "Say no more." His gaze shifted back to Grant. "If y'all need more room to work, we've got a big table. You're more'n welcome to use it. I just put the kids down for their nap."

Snatching up his briefcase, Grant rushed out the door, his chest brushing against Ellie in the cramped space. He swept an arm around her shoulder, ushering her out as well. "You know what, we were only going to be here a few minutes before we headed out anyway, so we'll just head on out..." he jerked the door closed, jammed a key into the lock, and gave it a vicious twist. "No one has to worry about anything." Taking Ellie's wrist, he turned towards the stairs. Ellie cast a look at Mr. Tisdale, who stood sucking on his lower lip.

"Later, Ed!" Grant called, without turning around.

"Offer still stands if you want to join us for hot dogs later!" Mr. Tisdale called after their retreating backs as Grant tugged her towards his Prius, which she could now see was parked to the side in a dirt parking space, "You two have fun."

The car door slammed on his words as Grant issued her into the car. Ellie hugged her backpack to herself. Grant jammed the car into gear, and they sped towards Cleveland's downtown.

"Well, he seemed..."

"Annoying? Nosey? All up in my business?"

Ellie cut a look at him. "I was going to say friendly."

Silence loomed in the car and settled like pollen over them. Coughing into her hand, Ellie asked, "I take it you don't like him."

"He... hovers." He pulled into a parking spot beside the

Chapter 8

Chamber of Commerce. A bright red train caboose sat on a platform in front of them, a couple of giggling toddlers clambering over it as their moms leaned against the hoods of their cars watching and chatting nearby.

Turning towards him, Ellie studied him as he took in their surroundings. "I thought he was just being polite. He did invite us to his cookout after all and he didn't have to do that. Is he a stay-at-home dad?"

Glancing at her and then the railroad museum behind them and to the side of the Chamber, he nodded. "I think so. His wife is a professor at the university."

"Maybe he's lonely." She lifted her hands at his skeptical look. "Aaaand, people in the South like to talk and tell stories. It's our way of making people feel welcome."

He opened his door. "Yeah, well, when it's ten at night and I just need my sink to stop dripping, I don't need his life story."

She rolled her eyes as she followed him. "And that right there is your problem."

"My what?" He spun to face her.

She heeled up to keep from colliding with his broad chest. The chest that was now heaving a few inches from her face. Looking up at him, she quirked an eyebrow. "Simmer down, boy." With a poke, she made him back up. "You asked for my help, remember?"

He crossed his arms and tilted his head. Oh. They were doing this now. She hadn't expected to be giving him an assessment of his character in a parking lot outside the Cleveland Chamber of Commerce, but if that's what he wanted.

Hunching her shoulders, she launched into it, refusing to overthink her words. "People think you're curt. And rude.

And that you don't want to talk to them or get to know them. That you just want things from them." She'd heard it all over town in every store she'd been in or landowner she'd talked to. Midnight Bluff did not like Grant Emberson one tiny bit.

"I'm trying to help them!" He sputtered and waved his arms, face flushing. Pacing he ran his hands through his hair. "Can't they... Don't they see..." He walked over to a bench and sat down, burying his face in his hands. "I should just leave. No one wants me here. Nothing I do is going to matter."

The crack in his voice is what did it. Ellie's heart flipped and swelled then squeezed tight so fast she clutched her chest and gasped.

"No!" she squeaked. He squinted up at her and she plopped down beside him, working some moisture back into her suddenly parched mouth. "What I mean is, I know you're trying to help. You're making a difference even if they can't see it yet." Tentatively, she patted his knee. "We just need to work on your people skills a bit. We do things a bit differently here in the South. You gotta take it slow, like a courtship."

"Courtship?" The side of his mouth quirked up even as his eyes stayed flat, and Ellie felt the heat in her cheeks. But she was going to ride this metaphor until the engine gave out, so help her.

"Yes, you gotta ease into it. Get to know your person; learn where they came from and who their people are"

"Their people?"

"Yeah, their people. Their family—who they belong to, where they went to school, what football team they cheer for. Football is big. If you don't have a team, you should get one."

He blinked. "Family. Football." Sitting back on the bench, he chewed on the inside of his mouth. "This is sounding an

Chapter 8

awful lot like a date."

Ellie laughed. That's why she'd picked the metaphor. "We don't do business with people we don't know. If we don't trust you, we don't deal. Since you're not from around here, you've got a lot of catching up to do."

Looking up at the sky, he huffed. "So how do I 'court' these guys?" Grant shuddered. "That just sounds so…"

Ignoring his rolling eyes, Ellie answered. "Chat them up a bit when you see them around town. Ask how business is treating them. Maybe buy them coffee or lunch. Find out what they need *and help* them with it." She shrugged. "Then you make your ask. Around here, you got to give to get."

His brow wrinkled. "That's just a business deal with a lot of fluff." With a sniff, he looked at her, his eyes growing contemplative. "I didn't have to do all that 'courtship' stuff with you. When I asked for help, you just said yes."

Picking at a spot in her jeans that had frayed from hopping a barbed wire fence, she mulled his statement over. Midnight Bluff had saved her from going to an orphanage when her mom walked out; the Pearces had kept her from bouncing from foster home to foster home. She'd sell her soul if it meant saving the town.

"This is my home. The only family I have. I'll do anything for them." She blinked away the sudden mist in her eyes and forced herself to grin up at him. "Even if that means helping a rude grouch like you."

He grumbled, "I am not a grouch."

"Not helping your case here."

Uncrossing his arms, he waved at the caboose and railroad museum next to them. "I have to admit that this is neat. I had no idea all this was here."

Surprised, she looked back at the laughing kids. The railroad museum was just the starting point of their day. "You haven't gotten out that much, have you?"

"I mean, I've been around Midnight Bluff. But there's not that much…"

Groaning, she stood, tugging on his wrist. "C'mon." She pulled him towards the Chamber of Commerce. "Today, we're meeting with the Chamber president then touring several of the museums and meeting with a couple of key shop owners so you can see how the Chamber supports members in a rural community. Get that noggin' of yours working again."

She waved an arm in a big arc. "Several years ago, Cleveland started the 'Keep Cleveland Boring' campaign which is this cool series of festivals and…" she glanced over her shoulder at Grant. He was grinning at her as she towed him towards the small grey Chamber building, and she smiled back at him.

Relaxing, she slid her hand down into his and pulled him inside as she continued her explanation. He had a good heart, and that she could trust even if the outside needed a little polish. There was so much she needed to show him about the Mississippi Delta, but she knew she could make him see how beautiful her home was.

Chapter 9

They'd claimed a table on the patio of Hey Joe's at the end of Cotton Row with an amazing view of the walking green and downtown shops over an hour ago. The table was covered with their notebooks, laptops, and corn chips, and a light breeze ruffled the pages and leaves of the greenery tucked into the nooks and crannies around them.

As late afternoon light filtered through the beams high above them, Ellie took a sip of her margarita from Mosquito Burrito, Hey Joe's sister restaurant next door, then patted her stomach in satisfaction.

"This is how you do a business lunch!" She reached across the table and punched Grant's arm. "See! If you just talked to everyone the same way you're talking to me now, you wouldn't have any problems."

He rolled his eyes at her, a move she already recognized as his signature, and dipped another chip in salsa. "If I'd known that all it took was a burrito and two margaritas to have my way, then I'd have pursued this course of action a long time ago."

"Aaaand we're back to pompous ass mode again." She took another sip of her margarita.

Eyeing her above his own drink, he scowled. "Maybe you should slow down on those."

"I'm good, Dad, thanks." She flipped back a few pages in her notebook. "Ok, so we've decided that a website where everyone can find out the goings-on of the town is definitely on the list. And we've got a weekly farmer's market during the summer. And repairing the brick streets and relandscaping the community green." Smiling, she looked up at him. "Pending you being able to pull a few strings to get us that grant money we need to do it right."

Grant made finger guns and a *click* sound at her. She suppressed a smile. The margarita was hitting him harder than he was letting on.

"Then, we want to try to do *both* a Spring and a Winter Festival?" Her voice wobbled. This was a lot to put together. Maybe they should be taking baby steps.

Leaning forward, he lowered his voice conspiratorially. "Two words: Ladies Auxiliary."

"Ooh. I like the way you think. Get someone else to do the real work while we 'delegate.'"

He pounded the table. "Hey! Delegation takes skill. You got to know things… people."

"Timetables." She pointed at him. "Timing is very important." She liked the way he thought, the straightforward way he tackled projects with vim. And gusto. And she needed to lay off on the margaritas after all.

"Very important." He took another sip of his margarita and set it on the table, condensation dripping onto the wood. "I'm

Chapter 9

so glad you brought me here. This place is so inspiring. Thank you."

For a minute they grinned stupidly at each other. Warmth blossomed in Ellie's chest as she gazed into his hazel eyes, and she cleared her throat. Tequila. It was the tequila. Whatever it was, it had her buzzing down to her fingertips, and she liked it. She took another sip.

"Ellie." Grant's face had become serious again, a line appearing between his eyebrows. "Can I ask you a question?"

She snickered. "You just did."

He rolled his eyes and laid his palms on the table. Eventually, he was going to sprain an eyeball doing that. Was that even possible? "Whatever. Forget it." He frowned at her, oozing grumpiness.

"Hey. I'm sorry." She sat forward and touched his hand with her fingertips. "Of course, you can ask me something."

Looking at her for a moment, he nodded. "I've traveled all over. Dealt with all kinds of people. And no one has thought me... rude before. Why here?"

She mulled the question over. It was odd. By all indications, Grant was successful in his field, but he'd bombed here. "I dunno. Maybe you just don't 'fit' here?" He raised his hands in frustration, making her fingers slide off, and she hurried to add. "I don't mean it like that! It's…" She searched for the words, staring at her palms, spread open like a book in front of her. The callouses ringing the inside of her thumbs and running across her palms from hoeing her little back garden caught her eye.

Holding out her hand, she pointed to bumps and scars running across it. "I guess what I mean is people don't take you seriously with your soft hands and Wonder Bread skin.

You don't *look* like you've done a day of work in your life."

He glanced at his hands self-consciously then put them in his lap. She bit her lip. "Now, I know that's not true. The things you do... The projections, the grant work, the profit and loss sheets, and investor pitches. Those aren't easy things. They take skill and they're incredibly draining. But it's invisible to most people around here. They need to see physical results before they'll believe anything."

"Am I supposed to get out with a pickaxe and fix the streets myself?"

She guffawed, and he tilted his head. "I'd love to see you do that. But no. I don't have any advice for you. I just think it might help for you to know how some people perceive you." Taking a breath, she added, "And to know that not everyone thinks that way." She dropped her eyes. "I mean, I'm impressed by you and all that you're doing."

"Ah." They drifted into silence, not quite as comfortable as before as Grant stared at the clouds overhead, considering. Scared she'd hurt his feelings, Ellie broke a chip into smaller and smaller pieces, obliterating it to dust.

A flicker of movement behind Grant caught her attention. A tiny bird, no larger than a sparrow darted between the beams. She squinted at it. "Is there something on my face?" Grant swiped at his mouth with a paper napkin.

"I'm not looking at you." She pointed, and he spun, nearly falling off the bench.

"I don't see anything."

"The bird."

"What bir... Oh." He glanced back at her, as she pulled her camera from her backpack. "Are you an ornithologist or something?"

Chapter 9

She laughed as she zoomed in on the tiny flickering creature. Flashes of yellow appeared in her lens. "Nope. Just really love birds." Adjusting her focus, she clicked the shutter. "And this one happens to be a lovely Myrtle Yellow-Rumped Warbler."

"Looks like a sparrow to me."

She chunked a balled-up napkin at his head. He caught it with a grin. "Sorry, couldn't resist. So, what makes this bird so cool?"

Happily, she leaned over the table to show him the picture and explain. As he listened to her gush about the merits of warblers, she breathed in the heady scent of his cologne, the sweet but somehow manly scent of orange blossoms. And something deeper, richer. She inhaled again. Sandalwood. It made her feel like she was in a Floridian orchard.

Resting his chin in his palm, he gazed at her. "You know so much about... everything around here." He stared at her, fascination writ large in his eyes. Heat flushed her cheeks.

"Just comes with the territory, I guess." She fiddled with her camera, playing with the aperture, then snapped a picture of him on a whim. "You look so serious!" Laughing, she showed it to him.

One side of his mouth hitched upwards. "You caught my good side."

She looked up at him. "I don't think you have a bad one. Being a bit serious isn't a bad thing."

He fiddled with her camera strap, and suddenly she was aware of how close they were sitting, their heads only a few inches only apart as they looked at the picture on her tiny screen. The sheer physical size of him, so close that if she just looked up, she could...

Sitting back, she planted her butt firmly on her bench and

pressed her lips together. He was still looking at her, the early afternoon sun dancing in his eyes. "I mean, I get pretty intense about my job too. So, I understand. Is what I'm saying."

Her throat went dry, and the entirety of the English language deserted her. "Mmm..." *Mmm?* This is what she was reduced to? She was beyond forming even proper syllables at this point.

The side door of Hey Joe's popped open, and Jackie Allen-Glower bounced out in bright pink nurse scrubs, hair up in a loose ponytail. Ellie waved way too enthusiastically, relieved for the distraction from her sudden inability to form coherent words.

Jackie didn't seem to notice her sudden spaziness. "Hey, sugar! Whatcha working on?" She strolled over, bags of to-go food hooked over her arm.

Grant patted Ellie's arm. "Big plans for Midnight Bluff!"

"Love it!" Jackie turned her hundred-watt smile on Grant who sat staring at the tall, pretty blond in fascination. A pang of jealousy ran through Ellie. Or it was heartburn. Had to be heartburn with how much she had just eaten. "Our little town is due for an upgrade."

Grant extended an arm. "I'm Grant... Have we met? You seem familiar." Feeling left out, Ellie watched the two of them shake hands.

"Oh, sugar, I'm sure we've seen each other around. I work for Dr. Washburn, so I'm in Cleveland as much as I'm in Midnight Bluff."

"You're the receptionist!" He pointed in triumph.

A stunned look crossed Jackie's face. "What? I'm not..."

Reaching for his arm, Ellie pushed it down. "Pompous ass alert!" she muttered to him. The last thing they needed to do was insult Jackie. She'd had a rough enough year with her

Chapter 9

husband Van's arrest a few months ago.

Grant glanced at her as if remembering she was there. "You're right." He took a breath. "I'm sorry. I called the office the other day to speak to Dr. Washburn about his cotton silo, and I believe you're the one who answered."

"His silo?" Ellie asked while Jackie laughed. A memory of Dottie's face clicked in the back of her mind.

"Oh, that!" Jackie swept her ponytail over her shoulder. "I was filling in for the receptionist while she was out with a sick kid, and I…" Her smile faded briefly. "I've been picking up all the hours I can since…" She waved her hand as if clearing cobwebs, smile back in place. "Anyway. Your out-of-town number made me think 'telemarketer.' We've been getting so many of those, we're all just over them." Waving at her outfit, she winked. "But no, as you can see, I'm a nurse."

"Gotcha." He bobbed his head in a friendly nod and looked over at Ellie, winking at her. "And where are you from?" Yep, that margarita was hitting him way harder than he thought.

Jackie laughed. "Midnight Bluff, sugar." Her smile grew bigger. Whether it was heartburn or jealousy, Ellie found herself waving a hand in front of Grant's face as he smiled back. Very maturely, waving, of course. In the most, non-attention-seeking way possible.

"Silo?" she asked again, as he blinked at her.

"Oh. The big cotton silo right on the edge of town. That would be perfect for a 'Welcome to Midnight Bluff' mural. It's in my notes. It belongs to Dr. Washburn."

Because *of course* it did. The most curmudgeonly old bachelor in Midnight Bluff just had to own the building Grant had his heart set on. Ellie sighed. They were going to have to bribe the old man with food; she just knew it.

"Jackie," she drawled the word. "Do you think Dr. Washburn would be interested in talking to us about a little paint job?"

Jackie bit her lip. "Not if you ask to meet with him." She glanced at Grant. "And definitely not if you ask." Her eyes lit up. "But he owes me." She pulled out her phone. "Hold on one sec." She punched in a number. A minute later, she held the phone out to Ellie and mouthed "Make it quick."

"Hey! Dr. Washburn. Ellie Winters." A grumbling huff met her ear. "I just need a minute of your time to go over a proposal that I have from Mayor Patty regarding your cotton silo."

She looked at Jackie's face, pinched in anxiety, and winked. He hadn't hung up on her, despite some very loud grumbling, which was a good start.

"Which silo?" She heard the slam of a door in the background and the squeak of a chair. The ole' coot was going to play tough to get.

She answered, voice steady, "The silo on the town line."

"Oh! My silo, you mean."

"Yes, that silo, the only one you own." She knew the properties in Midnight Bluff like the back of her hand, and Dr. Washburn's family had been on the same property for four generations.

"Don't get smart with me, young lady. You're already on thin ice getting my nurse to call me."

She smiled, knowing he liked when people argued back with him. They'd debated many times over pancakes at Al's Diner. He would just plop himself down in her booth and proceed to ask her opinion on some random current event and then take the opposite stance just to get on her nerves. "You know you like hearing my voice. And this time, if you hear me out, I'll owe you some pancakes."

Chapter 9

He paused, the quiet line crackling with interference. "Make it tomorrow morning at six sharp. I have to be in the office early." The phone clicked.

She grinned at Grant as Jackie hugged her. "We got the meeting." With a whoop, Grant reached over for a high-five.

Jackie glanced at her watch and waved at them. "Ok, gang, I've got to get lunch back to the office! Call me tomorrow, El, and let me know how everything goes. I know Doc won't say anything." She bounced off, Grant's eyes following her. Curling her toes in her shoes to keep from doing anything else stupid, Ellie jammed a tortilla chip into her mouth. And managed to stab her gum. Because she had no coordination today.

"She's nice." Grant finally turned back to grin at Ellie.

"Yep." Not wanting to talk about the all-around sweet and perfect Jackie, Ellie did what she did best: focused on work. "Ok, so tomorrow when we meet with Dr. Washburn, let me do the majority of the talking."

Grant nodded, "Sounds solid."

"We'll use this as a training run so you can see how Southerners like to interact. All you have to do is shake his hand and ask how he is."

"And let you take it from there." His eyes were dancing in the afternoon light and a smile crept across his face. It was so disarming, she nearly slid off the end of her bench.

"Huh? Oh, yes." She straightened and glanced back at her notes to keep from staring at him. "Exactly. I'll take it from there."

"Speaking of silos," she added, before she could lose her nerve, "A friend asked about something to do with hers the other day."

Grant leaned forward, his grin widening. "I don't think we can do murals everywhere. Much as I like to paint."

The thought of him in tight jeans and wielding a dripping paintbrush made her cheeks flush. "Not for a mural. She wants to Airbnb them."

"Huh. Didn't see that one coming. Not sure Airbnb does silo rentals for farmers."

Ellie shook her head and explained Dottie's concept. "She got it off of Pinterest," she ended. Grant looked intrigued.

"You know, there are lots of little places like that around here. And those sharecropper shacks… that's gold. An amazing way to tie in cultural heritage. Maybe even do a little historic preservation." He began scribbling notes on a legal pad. "I wonder if there's enough to do a rural tourism push." Drawing some circles around a few things, he reached for his laptop.

"Rural tourism? There's such a thing?" Ellie's fingers began buzzing as she reached for her phone to look it up. With the festivals they had planned, suddenly their ideas didn't seem so crazy.

"Oh yeah. People in cities want to get away from the hubbub, reconnect with the country and a simpler life. All that jazz." Grant waved a hand. "Could be a really good angle to go with. Midnight Bluff's got a great homey vibe to it. And the bayou and forest could be a big draw for outdoorsy types." He eyed her boots, covered in a film of mud.

Diving for her notes, Ellie began jotting down all the places that could be redeveloped. The old cinema was at the top of her list. Then the derelict train depot and the old gas station. She'd seen some cool renovations in Jackson the last time she'd been down to visit her cousin and jotted their names to look up: the Capri theater, the Ice House venue, the Iron Horse

Chapter 9

grill, and Ed's Burger Joint. Then there was Shack-Up Inn in Clarksdale—which may have been where Dottie got her true inspiration.

A buzz from her phone saved her from going full boss-babe mode. A potential buyer was waiting outside the catfish plant and wanted to see it NOW. Scooping up her stuff, she dumped it into her bag. Why didn't anyone ever schedule these things—especially out in the middle of nowhere in the Delta?

"Gotta go! Client." Pretending that it didn't mean that she might not be able to buy groceries at the end of the week, she pulled out a twenty. Grant waved her off.

"This is on me. I've got plenty to work with."

Who was she to argue with good luck? "See you in the morning!" She was already jogging for the exit, doing math in her head. Grant's apartment was only a five-minute walk up the street from the restaurant, and Cleveland was fifteen minutes from Midnight Bluff. If she didn't pay attention to the speed limit and Officer Chase wasn't out today...

"Ellie!" She turned back to Grant. "For the record, It's amazing that you're so passionate about your home. Every town could use more people like you." He nodded, "And thank you for the pep talk. I think you're pretty impressive too."

Unable to control her smile, she nodded and ducked out the door. As she braced herself to see if she could sprint with a backpack on, her heart was already racing for a whole other reason. Tequila. Definitely the last of the tequila burning off.

Chapter 10

Grant was officially at a loss for what to do with himself. He could just go back to his apartment... and walk straight into a tedious barbecue filled with screaming children and prying questions from his landlord. Nope, not even an option. But what did that leave him to do the rest of the afternoon? He and Ellie had knocked out so much, it was basically just spiffing it up now.

Pancakes. Ellie had mentioned owing Dr. Washburn pancakes and it was giving him a vague idea. Grant was beginning to think every business matter around here needed a certain amount of carbs and sugar to seal the deal.

Grateful for an excuse to do something other than dodge Ed and mope in his apartment staring at spreadsheets, he swept all of his papers off the increasingly sticky picnic table and hustled to his car. Exactly fifteen minutes later, he pulled up in front of the Loveless Bakery.

At the tinkling of the bells, Ruffin and Willow, suspiciously close together, looked up at him in surprise from the counter.

Chapter 10

Ruffin leaned against the front, studying him as Willow hastily began wiping down the already spotless glass top. Grant smirked at her reddening face.

"Hey, Will! If you have a second during your *very busy day*, I have a favor to ask."

Ruffin shoved his hands in his pockets and shuffled to the side, pretending to study the pastries in their cases. Slapping her rag down on the counter, Willow set her hands on her hips. "I'm extremely busy, Grant! What do you want?"

His grin widened as he turned in a slow circle and surveyed the deserted little bakery. "Business is just booming."

Ruffin cleared his throat. "I'll take a coffee to-go, please."

Willow arched an eyebrow at him.

"And a dozen croissants," he muttered. She nodded and grabbed a pastry box, folding it into shape with precise turns.

Grant stood, arms crossed, bemusedly watching as she delicately placed each croissant inside with a pointed look at him. Ruffin's shoulders rolled forward, the muscles straining against his shirt. Finally, she set his cup of coffee on top and pointed him towards the door.

He reached for his wallet. "I have to pay..."

"On the house." She pointed and Ruffin scurried outside like a scalded cat.

Grant leaned against the counter. "You've got him well trained."

Her shoulders shook with silent laughter, her short-cropped hair swinging around her ears. "Don't tell him that. He'd be mortified."

"Eh. He needs to get over it."

Her eyes glanced towards the door, a line appearing for a second between her brows before she smoothed her face and smiled. "What can I do for you, now that you're here?"

Grant studied her for a second longer, then dropped it. No need to go poking any sore spots. "Ellie mentioned something about owing Dr. Washburn some pancakes if he would meet with us and it got me to thinking that maybe I should take some pastries to—"

She cut him off, "Nope. Not a good idea."

He huffed. "I didn't even get to finish!"

"Because I know what you're going to say!" She threw up her hands. "And trying to bribe the business owners with coffee and pastry to listen to you would have worked if you had done it before you'd gone and pissed them off." She shook her head and crossed her arms. "Now it's just going to look like you're sucking up."

"But I am." He cleared his throat at the unexpected whine in his voice. "I'm trying to help them."

"Trying doesn't count as much as doing."

"That's what you keep telling me, but I'm not here to rebuild the town brick by brick by myself. I'm here to create the plan for them to do it themselves."

"Well then, you've got a catch-22, don't you?" She leaned her hip against the counter and sighed. "Look, Grant, I'm not telling you to do it all by yourself. But you've been in here just about every day for months complaining about the same thing, asking me what you should do. And I've yet to see you do more than spitball ideas and plug numbers into spreadsheets." She tapped the glass countertop. "It's time to stop complaining. Either quit or make a move."

Grant straightened, guilt lancing through him. She was right. At any other project, he'd have forced something to happen by now. But he'd sat here paralyzed ever since things hadn't

Chapter 10

worked with Cress. It was time to act. He jerked his chin in a shaky nod. "You're right."

He drew a hand over his face. "It's time to make some moves." She was watching him with squinched eyes. "Thanks for the advice. And the wake-up call." He tried to chuckle as he backed toward the door. "Maybe I can kick Ruffin for you sometime."

She laughed. "Maybe. Might do you more good than him though."

As he turned to leave, something about her words nagged at him. Pausing at the open door, bells jangling overhead, Grant looked back at her as she was about to disappear into her back room. "Willow, what do you think of me?"

She looked at him, eyes crinkled at the corner. "Why do you ask?"

He cleared his voice, throat suddenly dry. "I've heard that… some people don't trust me because I'm not a farmer, I wasn't born here." He looked down at his fist clenched around the doorknob. "That I'm too soft to get anything real done."

Shaking her head, she bit her lower lip. "I'm not from around here either, but for what it's worth, I think you have a good heart and good intentions." She inhaled through her nose. "People get to see me baking, sweating at the ovens. Maybe for you, people just need to see you getting out and rolling up your sleeves to help them. They can't always see or understand what you do in your office."

He drummed his fingers on the doorknob. "I guess that's the problem to tackle then."

She smiled. "I have every confidence you'll figure it out."

Laughing, he turned to go. "That makes one of us."

As he strolled down the sidewalk, Grant turned over Ellie and Willow's words in his mind. Passing one of the abandoned lots, he stopped and stared at it.

This one was a particular eyesore. Revulsion shivered over him. Last season's dull grass poked up through cracked concrete and piles of broken brick and cinder block teetered precariously, threatening to spill onto the sidewalk. Between the piles, trash had drifted in and melted into the crannies, creating a patchwork of faded newspaper, cardboard, and beer bottles that reeked of feral cats and dumpster sludge anytime the sun struck it. Which was every day between 10 AM and 3 PM. He gagged a little as the wind turned his way and hurried on.

If he couldn't even convince Herb to clean up these lots—

Grant stopped short on the sidewalk. Herb hadn't said no to cleaning up the lots. Just that he didn't have the time to do it himself. A half-baked idea began to spin in his mind. He sucked in a breath.

He couldn't do something that big without... asking anyone. Could he? He looked back at the lot, sitting putrid and baking in the sun, then at the courthouse, where even Mr. Pearce had nearly refused to do his job and help him. And suddenly, he was just done jumping through hoops at other people's whims.

If they wanted him to roll up his sleeves, by golly, he was going to do it. It might get him sent packing, but at least he'd go out with a bang. And these people would catch just a glimpse of what this town could be when someone fought for it.

Chapter 11

Ellie swiped at her eyes, again, and groaned. Why had she agreed to a 6 AM meeting? Grant grinned at her from the passenger seat, an adorable dimple she wanted to poke appearing in his cheek, and handed her a travel mug of coffee. Dimples and coffee. Ok, she could get used to this.

She yanked her eyes to the road. Nope. No. No way. Grant was a colleague. Not even really a friend. More a looky-loo in the grand scheme of things. She couldn't go and get any bad ideas about someone who wouldn't be here in six months. Or six weeks.

Her mind played tricks on her when the sun wasn't fully up. Grant snapped his fingers. "You in there, El?"

She bit her lower lip. And now they were apparently at the nickname stage.

He raised an eyebrow. "El?"

She needed to caffeinate, quick, before her brain got out of hand. Liquid hotter than the backside of the sun scalded her tongue, jerking her awake with a wince. "Huh? Oh, yeah. Just not one for mornings." She forced a laugh. "But the coffee's helping. Thank you." She had to get herself together.

A chocolate chip muffin appeared in front of her. Grant grinned at her, the dimple in full force. "I figured some sugar and carbs might be in order." Warmth flooded her cheeks at his thoughtfulness as her mouth watered. God, he was perfect.

With a shake, she forced herself to focus. "Sadly, I think that's going to have to wait for a few minutes." She turned onto a gravel drive. "We're here."

Grant scrambled to put everything away then flipped the mirrored visor down to swipe at his hair, neatening up his part. Laughing, Ellie reached over and grabbed his wrist. As she looked into his eyes, he stilled.

"You look fine. Just relax and enjoy getting to know someone new." She made a face as she accidentally brushed her fingers against his hair. "And maybe lay off the pomade."

His throat worked up and down as he stared intently at her. "I'll try." His other hand slid over the top of hers. "Thank you. For coming with me."

She nodded, aware of how small the cab of her truck was. "Of course." Pulling her tingling hand away, she swung open the door. "Now, let's go get that mural signed, sealed, and delivered for Mayor Patty!"

Dr. Washburn stood leaning against the side of his old steel-bodied Cadillac, arms crossed over his chest. As Ellie popped out of the truck, she wondered how he managed to keep such a heavy car so polished and clean on these dusty backroads.

"'Bout time you got here, girl!" he called out. He sauntered a few steps towards the silo, even his walk looking crisp in his starched and ironed scrubs.

Chapter 11

She glanced at her watch. It was 5:58. They were two minutes early. "And it's about time you stopped calling me girl, doncha' think?"

He walked over to her and hugged her. "What's with the stiff you brought with you?"

Glancing behind her, she spotted Grant standing stock straight beside her truck, hands clasped behind him. Sighing, she waved him over.

"I made him promise to be on his best behavior and I'm afraid it's gone to his head."

"If he's got anything up there to work with, I'll be da..."

"Doc!" she glared at him.

"Alright!" he held up his hands. "Not my first time dealing with a Yank. I'll play nice."

Grant reached them and held out his hand, arm straight as an arrow, to Dr. Washburn. "Nice to meet you, Doctor. I'm Grant Emberson. Thank you for meeting with us on such short notice."

Dr. Washburn shot Ellie a bemused look as Grunt pumped his hand up and down. "Call me, Clay. And it was my pleasure. Besides, there were pancakes on the line."

With a wink, Ellie waved at the silo looming over them. The corrugated metal structure was impressive, easily thirty feet across at the base and highly visible from the road.

"I bet this shines bright as a new penny on a sunny day." She turned to gaze up at it. The trick now was to get the good doctor to think it was his idea to paint a sign on the side of it—and he was sharp as a tack.

Shrugging, Dr. Washburn crossed his arms over his chest again. "Had to put new siding on it couple years back after that tornado blew through here. Lucky the whole thing didn't come down." He pursed his lips and studied her.

The problem was they knew each other's tactics too well. They had debated over breakfast at Al's so many times, she knew his tells and he knew hers. She debated. Boldness was called for in this situation.

"How far down the road can you see that thing anyway?" She crossed her arms as well and leaned toward him conspiratorially. Good to his word, Grant stood silent, hands clasped behind his back, eyes lit with curiosity as he looked back and forth between them.

Running his tongue over his teeth as he tried not to smile, Dr. Washburn scrubbed the toe of his tennis shoe through the gravel.

"Jes' about halfway near to Cleveland. Sucker's pretty big. Saw a crop duster that wasn't paying attention nearly take the top off it one day."

Laughter pealed out of Ellie, and she saw Grant startle, looking at her wide-eyed. "I bet that was a sight."

"He went wobbling off into the wide blue yonder. Poor fella' nearly had a heart attack." Dr. Washburn grinned at her then sobered. "But you didn't come out here to swap stories."

"No." She shook her head and gestured at Grant. "We're working on the town revamp project for Patty. And Patty's got her eye…" she pointed at the silo "… on a big 'Welcome to Midnight Bluff' mural that would look great right there."

"Why a corn silo?" Dr. Washburn scratched at his chin. "Why not just put up one of them big metal signs?"

Ellie nodded to Grant, who cleared his throat. "We want to capture the town's personality. Its charm. A metal sign wouldn't do that—it's soulless."

Working his jaw back and forth, Dr. Washburn stared at the

Chapter 11

silo. "I kinda like the idea, but..."

Ellie jumped as her phone rang. Glancing guiltily at the screen, her heart sank as she saw MR. STEVENS pop up on the Caller ID— he had to be calling for an update on the catfish plant.

"Sorry," she mouthed to Grant and slipped away back to the truck. Worst timing ever. Panicked, she hit the Answer button as she stared over the hood to where Grant and Dr. Washburn stood talking. Grant could pull this off without her. Miracles could happen.

* * *

Grant scratched the back of his neck as he stared at Dr. Washburn. They had not prepped for this. Ellie was supposed to be doing all the talking and now she was hung up for however long on a phone call. He looked over at her, widening his eyes in a silent, panicked plea. From the car, she shrugged helplessly at him.

Must be some phone call. He took a deep breath and turned to Dr. Washburn. Who was already scowling at him.

This was going great.

"A'ight." Dr. Washburn shifted his stance. "I know this is your little passion project." He bobbed his chin at Ellie. "Now that the lady isn't doing the speaking, let's get down to brass tacks, just you and me."

Grant scratched his chin. What in the hay were brass tacks? He nodded anyway, trying to go along with it. "Of course. What do you want to know?"

"I got a renter. Steady. Don't give me any trouble and don't tear the place up." He narrowed his eyes at Grant, sending a shiver down his back. "Respectful." Letting the word hang for a second, Dr. Washburn sucked in his upper lip assessing Grant.

Grant cleared his throat. "Got it. So, you want...?" He realized he didn't know what Dr. Washburn meant. Did people actually rent silos out here?

"I don't want anything that might..." Dr. Washburn gestured to the silo. "...happen, to get in the way of their use or access. This is a working silo after all. And it's going to stay working. Or no deal."

Sighing in relief, Grant nodded. "We can make that happen. I'm sure we can work around the harvest schedule and any other needs to get the mural done. And once it's complete, it will only need occasional touchups."

"I have your word on that?"

Without hesitating, Grant held out his hand. "I'll do you one better and put it in the contract when we get to that step." He forced a grin even as his heart stuttered.

Dr. Washburn eyed his hand, eyebrow cocked. "Jumping the gun there a bit. We haven't discussed materials or access to my property."

Slowly, Grant let his arm drop. "Of course." How was he making such amateur mistakes? Shaking his head, he added, "Sorry, just eager to make some progress."

With a knowing look, Dr. Washburn nodded. "I'm sure you are, from what I've heard. But 'round here, we like to take our time. Make sure we know who we're doing business with."

Grant crossed his arms as prickles of irritation ran across his chest. "In my experience, words don't mean much unless you mean it enough to put it in writing too. You can know

Chapter 11

someone for forty years and they can still pull the wool over your eyes if you're not careful." His mind flitted to Bo's party last fall as he searched for an example to help him make his point. "Just look at Mr. Glower, fleecing half the county."

Dr. Washburn flinched, but his face hardened. "If you go around calling everybody stupid for trusting their neighbor, no wonder you haven't been making any headway, son."

At the diminutive title, Grant clenched his fists. Bringing up Mr. Glower may have been a low blow, but he was the perfect example of why contracts were necessary. And acknowledging this fact didn't make Grant immature or skeptical. It made him smart—as evidenced by the number of landowners around here who'd gotten cheated, shafted, and outright stolen from by just one person.

He stood up straighter. Nope, he was tired of getting talked down to and taken less seriously because he was a "Yank" and a "city-slicker" who couldn't possibly understand a country way of life.

"I call it like I see it." He shrugged. "And if folks don't like it, that's on them. Doesn't undo the fact that contracts can help keep good neighbors as good neighbors."

Rubbing his wrist, Dr. Washburn breathed deep. "They told me I was crazy to talk to you. That you didn't get how we do business. And they were right. If that's what you think of us, then we're done talking here."

With that, he turned on his heel and swung back into his car, slamming the heavy metal door. As the car scratched off down the drive, Grant lifted his hands and asked the receding tailpipe. "Who is 'they'?" All he was rewarded with was a brief flash of red brake lights as Dr. Washburn swung from the gravel of the drive onto the concrete of the highway.

Behind him, an irate voice piped up. "What did you say?" He turned around to see Ellie staring up at him, hands on her hips and eyes glittering with anger.

* * *

Two minutes. She had been on the phone for two minutes and in that amount of time, Grant had not only managed to anger Dr. Washburn and put their deal in jeopardy. But he'd also burned any chance they'd had with him to the ground.

She was going to owe Dr. Washburn pancakes for a month. And she could not afford that.

Pinching the bridge of her nose, she took a deep breath. "Ok, let's go over this again, one more time. What, exactly, did you say?"

Grant slumped against the passenger side window as they sat in her truck talking over the disaster. "Do we need to go over this a third time?" He balled up the wrapper of his muffin and shoved it into the paper bag at his feet so forcefully she was surprised it didn't rip. "I essentially called the man a dumbass and insulted the 'honor' of his entire hometown to boot."

His sigh filled the entire cab as he slumped down further. "I might as well just hand in my resignation now and get on the next flight back to Wisconsin."

Ellie twisted her fingers together, willing her irritation with him and his obliviousness to simmer down. Taking a long sip of her now-cold coffee, she considered her words. "It's my hometown, too." Her words were quiet and measured.

Carefully, she balanced the cup between her knees as Grant sat up and looked at her. "I didn't realize…"

Chapter 11

She shook her head. "Most people don't. Not even a lot of people from here. My dad skipped town before I was born, and my mom just... well..." she waved a hand not wanting to get into it right now. "I was in and out of a lot of foster homes in Cleveland. When I was fifteen, Lou Ellen's family, the Pearces, took me in." She saw his mouth twitch and added. "And thank God for it, or I'd have been another teenage runaway. But yes, Midnight Bluff is my hometown."

Grant leaned toward her. "I'm sorry—I didn't mean..."

She shook her head again. "I've been in real estate for nearly ten years, Grant. So, believe me when I say I get it about contracts."

Turning to him, she laid a hand on his arm and looked him in the eye. "But you also have to understand just how much we trust our neighbors here. They're the ones who lend us tractors when ours break down right when the cotton comes in. They're there giving us the shirt off their back when a tornado rips through and destroys a house. Or the river floods."

His brow wrinkled in concentration as he slid his palm, warm and reassuring, into hers. "Yes, you'll find... people... anywhere who'll get twisted. But I'm living proof of the good that's here too. That's why we give our word. Because often, a man's word is all he has here."

As her words hung in the air, Grant rubbed his thumb across the back of her hand once. He searched her eyes, and for a split second, the air warmed between them as if he were about to kiss her. Her chest lifted in anticipation.

Then he jerked his chin in a slight nod and leaned back into his seat, his palm sliding from hers. "Ok." He stared out the window, his hand clenched in his lap. "I trust. If you say to take someone at their word, then I will."

Ellie's shoulders sagged. What was wrong with her, letting her mind run away from her like that? With a hoarse chuckle, she turned and jammed the key into the ignition, having to try twice before she got it in. "Good, cuz I can't keep giving you crash courses on how to be Southern. Some of this stuff you just have to pay attention to and pick up on your own."

He smirked at her. "But you make such a great teacher."

She pointed at him. "Keep saying things like that and I'm going to start charging you for lessons."

His smile widened. "Oh, and what's my fee going to be?"

Her stomach exploded into fizzy bubbles, and she shook her head tongue-tied. She concentrated on executing the world's most perfect, and unnecessary, three-point turn as they headed back down the drive.

"I'll just add it to your tab." She waved her hand in what she hoped was a breezy fashion.

Grant laughed. "I look forward to settling up later."

Was this… were they flirting? They couldn't be flirting. Flirting was always so cringy. This was just banter between co-workers. Yep. Just friendly banter.

She snuck a look at Grant and the perfectly chiseled line of his jaw. Her smokin' hot co-worker. Eyes on the road. That's what she needed to concentrate on right now. Keeping her eyes on the road.

As they rolled down the drive toward the highway, gravel popped and pinged under the tires. The sun was just cresting the trees in a delicate scrim of pink and gold as they rumbled over the pavement back into the heart of town, sudden silence between them. Had she imagined the moment back there—her overactive mind at play?

Glancing at him out of the corner of her eye, she noted the

Chapter 11

smooth curve of his shoulder, the way he rested his chin on his fist, brushing his thumb absently over his lips. He seemed perfectly at ease.

Grant interrupted her inner monologue. "Who rents from Dr. Washburn?"

"Huh?"

"Dr. Washburn said he had a renter. Do you know who it is?"

Ellie rubbed her lips together, feeling the last of her Chapstick working its way off. It wasn't her place to tell, but the info seemed harmless enough. "No one rents from him." Grant's face clouded with confusion. "He lets Jackie use the silo after the land that hers was on was seized by the IRS. After Van's arrest last year. She's doing her best to keep the house and farm that her grandparents left her."

With a groan, Grant plunked his forehead into his palm. "Oh." He sat there for a moment. "And I just insulted the man."

"Yep." She wasn't going to do anything to lessen his guilt. As much as she liked Grant, he had to learn how to talk to people around here on their terms. And she couldn't help him with that by bubble-wrapping his feelings. "Several of her neighbors have been taking turns helping her with what little land she's been able to keep. Betty Coleman, the council member, is one of them. Like I said, we look out for one another."

Grant's face softened. "I owe Dr. Washburn an apology."

"You could say that." She snuck another glance at him. "Maybe you could start by buying him a stack of pancakes. The man likes his carbs." And it could take some off what she owed him.

Grant nodded and shot her a weak smile. "So, you never answered. Do you think I should quit?"

The question made her jerk, the tires hitting the rumble strip and jolting them both upright.

"No!" The word shot from her gut to her lips before she could catch it, turn it into something less naked and instinctive. Blushing, she bit the inside of her cheek. "What I mean is, let's see how this meeting with Patty at the end of the week goes before you make any decisions."

He looked at her, incredulous, eyebrows rising in amusement up his forehead. "Because all my other meetings have gone so well."

"But you haven't known the secret before." She grinned at him as they pulled up in front of the Loveless Bakery.

"And that is?" he asked, his eyes twinkling at her.

"A little sweetness goes a long way," she sing-songed as she swung out of the truck, "And I'm the sweetest thing of all!"

His laughter followed her like the chiming of the bakery bells as they tramped inside to top off their coffee.

Chapter 12

Grant waved at Ellie as she whisked into her truck and whipped down the street. He knew she had showings and clients to take care of, but... His hand tingled from where her palm had rested in his earlier, the warmth seeping up his arm.

He shook his head. Nope. He was not going to get lost in a silly crush. He was going to march himself over to the courthouse, sit down at a desk, and get to work organizing his notes and researching other Mississippi towns with rural tourism programs and heritage campaigns. Yep. That was exactly what he was going to do.

Turning on his heel, he marched across the square and into the lobby, nodding a cheerful hello at a scowling Mr. Pearce. He wanted to know who put vinegar in that man's Cheerios. A high, nasally voice cut through the air behind him.

"Daddy!" Lou Ellen, an arm full of packages, clicked across the gleaming tile of the vestibule in her high heels and planted a kiss on her father's cheek as a rare smile lit up his face.

"Darling, what are you doing here?" He wrapped an arm around her waist and shot another scowl at Grant. So, it was just his presence that offended him. Great. Grant hunched his shoulders and tried to scooch around a corner, but the world just wasn't on his side today.

Mayor Patty bustled down the hallway, spotting him. "Grant!" Her voice echoed from the tile floor to the wooden beams soaring overhead. "Just the man I wanted to see."

Lou Ellen's eyes darted to him, her mouth pressing into a thin line. She turned away primly, her shoulders stiff and back ramrod straight. He'd just asked her out, nothing more. You'd think he'd gravely insulted her honor from the way she acted. He shook his head and rolled his eyes to the ceiling. Some people you just can't win over.

Patty's eyes hadn't missed a thing and she stood waiting for him, face sympathetic, as he walked over to her. She patted his arm before turning and motioning for him to follow her. "I've heard about you teaming up with Miss Winters and I have to say I'm pleased. That's a smart move."

Keeping his voice upbeat, he said, "We've already met a couple of times and have several exciting new directions to work on. I think you'll be pleased."

"As long as you can get some more people behind you, I'll support whatever you bring to me." She squeezed his arm then released him as they reached the door of her office. "And I've been thinking about the old railroad. I'd love to do something with it."

Grant nodded, trying not to scowl, as he glanced back at Mr. Pearce and Lou Ellen, who was now handing him what looked like a bag lunch. Mr. Pearce beamed at his daughter as she waved at him and called down the hall to Mayor Patty, "I left

Chapter 12

those packages in the storage room for you, Patty!"

With a smile, Patty called back, "Ok, sugar. Thank you."

"I didn't realize Lou Ellen worked here too." Grant glanced at Mayor Patty as they entered her office. Morning light glanced off the varnished top of her desk, what little he could see under the piles of paper.

"She does some errands for me here and there." Mayor Patty shrugged. "On slow days at the church, mostly." She stared out the window, a hand on her mouth as she murmured, "There hasn't been much for her to do lately."

Vaguely, Grant remembered something about Lou Ellen being the secretary there. He sat on the edge of a chair. "You said something about the old railroad?"

"Ah, yes." She leaned forward and pulled a map from the bottom of a stack of pages, causing the whole pile to lean precariously. "The old track. It's long out of use—the land has reverted to town ownership. I thought it might be interesting to do something with it."

She handed the map to him. He studied the page, narrowing his eyes as he looked over the faint markings. It was an incredibly thin plot that stretched from one side of Midnight Bluff all the way to Cleveland.

Tapping his lips, he hummed in his throat. "Are you wanting a public space or something to make revenue?" It was so small, his first instinct was to subdivide the land and sell the plots to the owners who already bordered those areas. If they wanted it. That might be a great way to end up with some patchy plots of scrub bushes and thorns.

Shrugging, Mayor Patty smiled. "That's up to you." She glanced at her watch. "Think on it and pitch me an idea or two at the next council meeting. I look forward to seeing how creative you can get with it."

"Next council meeting?" He stared at Mayor Patty.

She waved him out the door. "Oh yes, I figured I'd give you two time to mingle your ideas. Creativity takes time to percolate. I have every confidence you and Ellie will come up with something wonderful together."

Grant stood, his heart skittering. This was amazing. That was two whole extra weeks to put a plan together and get people on board. Forget Dr. Washburn. They could have half the town revved up and ready to go by then.

As the door closed behind him, his thoughts flitted to Ellie and her twinkling eyes. He bet she'd have a million ideas for a space like the old railroad track. A go-cart track or a wildflower garden—something fun and entertaining that would draw people in.

He stared at the map the mayor had given him as he walked back down the hall.

"You Grant Emberson?"

His head snapped up at the gruff voice. A man in muddy work boots, worn jeans, and a khaki shirt stood in the middle of the vestibule, chewing on something that Grant didn't want to contemplate. The man spat into an old fast-food cup.

Grimacing, Grant held out his hand automatically. "That's me. How can I help you?"

The guy smirked at him. "I've got your delivery." He jerked his thumb toward the front door.

Blinking, Grant looked at the door and the man and then back at the door before it clicked. "Oh! Yes. Thank you."

No time like the present to start showing these people what the future could look like. He tossed his briefcase and the rolled-up map onto a bench along the wall. Gesturing, he said,

Chapter 12

"After you."

The man chuckled. "They told me you was an odd one." But he headed gamely out the door. On the street in front of the abandoned lot, its scuffed yellow paint shining like a caution sign in the sun, was a loader with a backhoe. And taking up the entire sidewalk was a dented and rusted industrial dumpster. Grant wanted to fist pump. For about five seconds before he realized that he didn't know how to drive the dang thing.

The man stood scratching his beard and looking at him. He nodded his head at the lot. "You clearing that?"

A gust of wind smacked Grant in the face with a cloud of pollen. Coughing, all Grant could manage was a nod.

"Good. 'Bout dang time." The man slapped him on the back. "Do you need a how-to or are you good? I got more deliveries to run." He began shifting impatiently towards a flatbed truck.

Still coughing, Grant held up a thumb. He could YouTube it, right? The man slapped a key in his hand and sauntered off. Staring at the tractor, Grant immediately realized his mistake. He circled it slowly. It had looked so small on the website. Easy to figure out. Any nincompoop could do it. Just a few swoops with this thing and he'd show this sleepy little town all it took to come up in the world was determination—and some heavy machinery.

In real life, the backhoe towered above him in a steel arch of death. He swallowed as he realized he was going to kill someone, most likely himself. Or worse—punch a hole in a wall. He backed away a couple of steps. Nope, no way could he do this.

"Grant?"

His whole body cringed. The last person in the world he wanted to see right now stood behind him. And she was laughing her butt off.

"Cress." The word came out flat. God, she was laughing so hard tears were coming out of her eyes. He wanted to turn invisible. He wanted to turn into a vapor and float away on the wind back to Wisconsin. He wanted to melt into a puddle and slip between the cracks of the crumbling brick pavement. Instead, he waved an arm at the loader. "Really? You of all people laughing at me?"

She straightened and wiped at her face. "I'm sorry. I'm not…" She snorted. "I'm not laughing at what you're doing." He huffed, and she waved her hands. "I'm really not." She took a deep breath and let it out in a rush, forcing herself to stop. "I was laughing at the look of utter dismay on your face."

He rolled his eyes and took a step away from her. The last thing he needed was his ex—who humiliated him in public then made him come back for seconds at her wedding—to be making fun of him right now.

"Grant, wait!"

"Cress, I'm not doing this with you right now!" he snapped. "I've had enough of everybody in this town making fun of me, and I won't have it from you too." His eyes burned and he turned away.

"I was going to offer to help." Her voice was so quiet he almost missed it in the breeze that kicked up.

With a sigh, he turned back toward her. She stood staring up at him with those big green eyes. The ones that used to make him feel like he was a superhero. Like he was the only one in the world who mattered to her. He shook his head, trying to clear his racing thoughts.

"Unless you know how to drive one of these things…"

She nodded so hard he thought she'd turned into a bobble-

Chapter 12

head. "I do."

He stared at her. "Since... when?"

Plucking the key from his hand, she climbed up on the seat. "I'm a farm girl, remember?"

"Yeah, but..." The roar of an engine drowned him out. "I thought you hated power tools," he said into the bass rumble as the huge machine reared to life. The look of satisfaction on Cress' face made him trail off. She'd changed. The girl who used to be afraid of a power drill now rode atop a backhoe that he was scared to touch. He took a deep breath as she waved him up. Well, if she could change, he could too.

* * *

Carefully, Grant dumped a bucket full of crumbling cinder block and brick into the dumpster. The noise echoed through his chest and reverberated down into his toes. Maybe he should have gotten some earplugs. Too late now, he was committed to this. As the dust settled, he turned the tractor back to the neat pile of rubble he'd collected in the middle of the lot with the helpful instructions of Cress.

She leaned now against a faded STOP sign, watching him with a big grin plastered on her face, one hand across her forehead to shield her eyes from the sun. He waved at her as he slowly turned the hulking machine. He was still nervous about accidentally punching a hole in a wall, but so far so good.

As he scooped up another bucket of debris, he allowed himself to relax just a bit. Until he swung around. Herb stood next to Cress, arms crossed over his chest and eyebrows pinched in a scowl. Grant tensed and sent the arm of the backhoe clanging into the dumpster.

Scrambling for the controls, Grant quickly dumped his load and cut the machine. He leaped from the cab of the tractor. "Herb, I can explain!"

Cress elbowed Herb. "Quit it!"

A guffaw erupted from the man as he doubled over laughing. This was the second time today someone had burst out laughing at him. Grant stood thunderstruck. What was happening?

"Man! This is great." Herb grabbed his hand and pulled him into a tight hug. "How'd you even think of this?"

Grant flushed as Herb released him. Rubbing at the back of his neck, he pointed at the lot. "You didn't say that you didn't want the lots cleared." He glanced guiltily from Herb to Cress, who was grinning at him as well. "Just that you didn't have time to do it yourself." Shrugging, he shoved his hands in his pockets. "And with the way things were going, I figured why not take a chance on it myself?"

"So, you rented a dumpster?" Herb clapped him on the shoulder. "I love it!" He chuckled and gripped his shoulder, looking toward the courthouse. "But uh, I'm going to take over and finish this real quick. Since we don't have any permits. And are kinda blocking a public sidewalk. Don't worry. I'll let you have one last moment of glory at the end."

Herb swung up onto the big tractor and cranked it back up. "But I like the attitude. Not bad, Emberson!"

As the tractor rumbled back to work, Cress bumped his shoulder. "See, not everyone is so bad around here."

Grant cupped his chin. "Guess not." He glanced at her, gratitude washing through him. "Guess I just had to let go of my idea how things should be to see it."

Chapter 13

With a thunk, Ellie plopped her head back against the seat of her truck. Another dud. What was up with these buyers? Didn't they read the terms of the listing? Swiping her hands over her face, she pulled up the listing on her phone and reread. Yep, right there it said "to be sold in its entirety." So why these buyers kept thinking she'd try to work out a deal for them to get only the scrap metal was beyond her. Mr. Stevens was not going to be pleased. He wanted results, like, yesterday.

Listlessly, she swung open the door of the truck and trudged into the bakery, the grind and slam of construction echoing behind her. She didn't even bother turning around to look. The pipes must have gotten clogged at the courthouse again.

It took a second for her eyes to adjust to the dimmer light inside, but once she blinked, she saw Lou Ellen and Willow gaggled up at the cash register. Excited expressions lifted both of their faces.

"Congrats!" Willow squealed.

"You guys are awesome!" Lou Ellen wrapped her waist in a strangling hug.

Ellie gasped at the anaconda grip. She was used to Lou Ellen's enthusiasm, but this was another level. "What in the dickens are you talking about?"

"The lot!" Lou Ellen shrieked, pointing out the window. "That stinky eyesore."

"Grant..." Willow tried to explain.

"Grant did what?" Ellie asked, horrified as she spotted a giant green dumpster and a gathering crowd of pedestrians. Not listening to their squeaks, she rushed out the door, her backpack hanging awkwardly from her arm.

Across the square, she spotted Herb leaning against the one STOP sign. He looked puzzlingly unruffled even as a sweaty Grant dumped what looked to be the last of a significant portion of cinder block and brick into the dumpster.

She set down her backpack and turned to Herb. "Weren't you talking about salvaging that?"

He shrugged. "Yeah, but..." Waving an arm at the space as Grant cut the engine of the tractor, the sudden silence underlined the emptiness of the lot. The wide-open potential of the space. "A clean slate is just so much better than an unused pile of maybe."

Ellie couldn't help but nod. The white slab of concrete looked pristine compared to the heaps of rubble and trash that had been here just this morning. As Grant climbed down from the machine, he spotted her and smiled, that dimple appearing in his cheek. Unable to stop herself, she smiled back.

"Well, if this is the influence you have on him, I'd say it's a very good thing." Herb winked at her, leaving her feeling flustered, and sidled off just as Grant walked up.

Chapter 13

"What did Herb say?" Grant asked.

"Mmm…" She hunted for an explanation. "Just that he's happy with the clean space."

With a nod, Grant looked at it satisfied. "I can't go renting backhoes every day, but maybe this will inspire people a little." He drew a crumpled tissue from his pocket and blew his nose then tossed it into the dumpster.

Looking around at the crowd as people milled about the now open foundation and kids chased each other, Ellie nodded. "I'd say you did good." She held up a hand for a high five. "Real winner here."

Grant slapped his palm into hers and then let his hand linger as he turned to look back at the tractor and loader. "My dad is a real white-collar type—he wouldn't believe his eyes if he saw me now." He grinned at her. "But I think he'd be proud."

A pit opened in Ellie's stomach. She dropped her eyes and slid her hand from his. Her dad hadn't cared two cents about her much less been proud of her. As she shuffled away, Grant caught her sleeve. "Hey." He bent down to catch her eye. "I'm sorry. I didn't mean… I wasn't trying to be insensitive about your family. I'm honored that you told me what you did earlier."

Suddenly, her eyes were brimming. "Thank you." She inhaled through her nose. "I know you didn't mean anything by it." She chuckled. "It's just… a tender spot, ya' know?" Clutching her elbows, she murmured, "I've always wanted my own family. It just hasn't happened for me." She stared down at a crack in the sidewalk feeling as if she just handed him her heart.

Slowly, slowly enough that she could pull away if she wanted, he leaned over and hugged her. "I'm sure it will. You deserve the best." His warmth washed over, blanketing her in comfort and a sense of safety. She squeezed her eyes shut, not wanting it to stop. He squeezed a little then let her go, and with his presence the warmth.

She tried to tell herself that she wasn't disappointed, but that was a big, fat lie. Instead, she focused on the obvious. "When did you start caring what people around here think?"

He laughed. "When a certain real estate agent chewed me out about it!" She tried not to grin, losing the battle with her traitorous cheeks.

"Why if it isn't my almost son-in-law!" Ellie watched as Grant's shoulders shot up to his ears.

"Leora." A stiff smile etched itself onto his face, and Ellie turned to see an amused-looking Leora in a cotton sundress glancing between the two of them.

"Oh, do go on. I've interrupted something… important." She looped the handle of her bag around her forearm, the corner of her mouth inching up. Rumors would be around Midnight Bluff by nightfall if Ellie didn't do something fast.

"You're just the lady we needed to speak to." Grant cast a reproachful glare at Ellie as she drew Leora toward them by her elbow. "You see, we have this absolutely wonderful—marvelous really—idea on how to get Midnight Bluff on the map. But it needs just the right sort of person to make it happen. Someone with a magic touch. And, well, you are our resident miracle worker!"

Leora nodded thoughtfully. "True, true."

Grant opened his mouth, looking confused. Behind Leora, Ellie punched his arm. "So, we were thinking… festivals." With a theatrical wave of her arm, she turned Leora toward the empty square and launched into an impromptu pitch of the

Chapter 13

series of yearly music and makers festivals they wanted to host. "Midnight Bluff bustling and full of people—here to see something only we could offer. And you can help us make it happen."

Hands clasped under her chin, Leora stood, face aglow. Ellie had never seen her look so rapt. Even Grant had hushed, watching her features soften and lift. "Oh, Ellie! It reminds me of the old hymn sings from when I was a little girl. Before the trees died."

Leora grasped Ellie's arm, eyes shimmering. "People would bring their instruments to the square—guitars, harmonicas, banjos, even violins—and we'd sing the old songs." Laughter bubbled up, rich as caramel. "It wasn't all hymns mind you. There was a fair bit of blues, and we'd even slip some Elvis in there, but to be all together making music…" She blinked and shifted. "It was somethin' special." With a smile, she said, "I'd be honored to head this up. I'm sure the Ladies' Auxiliary would agree. Send me more details when you have them, and we'll take it from there."

Hugging her, Ellie whispered, "Thank you."

With a sniff, Leora straightened. "What are neighbors for?" Jerking her chin in a nod at Grant, Leora swept on down the sidewalk.

"She never stops surprising me," Grant murmured.

"And she never will." Ellie gazed after her, happy to have someone as formidable as Leora McBride behind them.

Picking up her backpack, Grant turned toward the courthouse and held his arm out in a mock show of courtliness. "Now, let's go get some inspiration ready for these other folks, shall we?"

She threw her head back and laughed. "We shall!"

Chapter 14

Ellie stared at the stacks of paper spread out on the conference table, amazed by the sheer amount of work Grant had put into understanding Midnight Bluff. He possibly understood the challenges facing her community better than she did. Shaking her head, she picked up one stack, skimming the xeroxed columns of numbers.

"Census data?" She asked.

"Tracking population shrink over the last several decades." Grant cleared a space on one end of the table. "That's not important right now though." Today he was wearing a button-up shirt, the sleeves rolled up to highlight his muscular forearms. Stubble swept over his jaw, and she longed to rub her fingers over it. She swallowed and looked back at the stacks of data.

"How's that not important? Without people..."

He squinted up at her, hands full of notes. "Because what's done is done. We can't plan for the future if we're overly fixated on the past. We learn what we need to from it, then we move

Chapter 14

forward." He muttered, "A lesson I need to start remembering."

Ellie walked slowly around the table, surveying the material. The bulk of it appeared to be from the archives. Tax revenue, land rolls, business logs, even crime rates lay spread out before her. With a little shock, she even recognized copies of certificates of sale for land and houses that she had sold. But among all the detritus there was nothing to indicate public sentiment or opinion on *what to do* about Midnight Bluff's economic status.

She sat down drumming her fingers. "Why are we doing this?"

"Excuse me?" Grant halted, mouth hanging open.

"No... I meant..." She gestured between them. "Why are you and I doing this alone? Why haven't other members of the community like Lester Chambers from Southern Comfort and Vada and Leora gotten on board earlier to help drive this? We should have stacks of data on what people think should be done—some sort of community feedback loop." This was as big of a blind spot as not including a Chamber of Commerce. Grant didn't seem incompetent—he'd tossed out some amazing ideas just yesterday—but she was beginning to wonder if something more was going on.

He sank into a chair, swiping his hands down his face. "That's a long story."

Clearing a pile from another seat, she settled in beside. "We have all night." He looked at her gratefully.

"You know, you're the first person to take the time to really talk to me since last fall. Besides Willow." He scrubbed at some dirt on his slacks. "It's... it's been nice."

Her heart clenched as she remembered him landing in the dirt, how he'd practically disappeared after that. She could only imagine the turmoil he'd gone through. And as an outsider in a small town.

"When all of that happened... I didn't handle it well. I got snappish. And the council, understandably, stopped listening to me." Grant shook his head, lips pressed together. "Worst possible timing. That was right when I was beginning to tabulate all my findings and realize just how deep Midnight Bluff's problem runs. It was incredibly important to get a feel for the community. And I found myself shut out." He looked down at his lap as he shoved his hands in his pockets.

Ellie swallowed. "We do tend to close ranks."

Grant laughed. "That's the polite way to put it." He cleared his throat. "Anyway, I lost my temper in a meeting. The meeting where I was supposed to be asking for approval for that community feedback form you just mentioned. I think Herb said something snippy about my tie or something and I just... lost it."

He paused. "You can imagine how that went." Ellie covered her mouth, trying not to laugh from horror at the image of strait-laced Grant going off on stoic Herb in his denim shirt and scuffed up boots. Grant sighed. "I was arrogant. And hot-headed. And deserved every word of the dressing down I got from Patty. God bless her, she's been the only one who's stood behind me through this." He clenched his fists. "But six months of being iced out by everyone else? I've made my apologies and still, no one will talk to me."

Resting his forearms on the table, he turned his palms up. A sheen glimmered in his eyes. "What am I supposed to do, El? This town doesn't have the capital to withstand the next thing that hits it—a tornado, flood. Heck, a sewer line breaking. And I can't do a dang thing about it because these people are too

Chapter 14

stiff-necked to let me help them."

Ellie pressed her hand to his shoulder. He flinched then relaxed. "I'm here now. We're a team and we're going to do this together." He stared at her, desperation pooling in his eyes. She searched for the words to buoy him. "Look at all you've managed to do on your own." She gestured at the table, covered in mountains of work she couldn't comprehend. "You did this. And all those people outside marveling at that empty lot—"

He scoffed and she shook him. "You did that. That was all your idea."

"It's just an empty clearing."

"That was filled with garbage. And now it's a blank slate they can see something being built in. That's hope, Grant. And you gave it to them."

"But it's just one thing—"

"One action is enough to set a whole chain of events in motion." When he shook his head again, she groaned. "Look, you idiot! Who did you do that action for?"

"Herb... so he would see that cleaning up his storefronts is a good idea."

"But Herb is the councilman you had a falling out with." She rolled her eyes. Were all men this dense, or just this one?

A light finally sparked in Grant's features. "So, you're saying that by doing this, I've patched things up with Herb?"

Finally, he was getting it. Ellie nodded. "Which will look good to the rest of the town, soften them up a bit." She squeezed his shoulder, marveling at the muscles hidden under his dress shirt. Jerking her eyes back up to his, she added, "And it gave us an opening with Leora. Two birds, one stone."

Grant sat back in his chair, breaking the contact between

them. "If only I could luck into such good ideas all the time."

Ellie crossed her legs. "Well, we can capitalize off this one some more."

He raised an eyebrow. "Oh, how?"

Sitting forward to the table, she grinned. "I've got a plan. And it involves that feedback form. We just need to modify it a bit."

Intrigued, he scooched his chair up, his knee brushing hers. "I like the way you think."

"Mmm. What else do you like about me?" She blushed up to her hairline as the words popped out of her mouth. She stared down at the notebook in front of her, shocked by her boldness. This was nothing like their banter in the truck. Her words were direct, an invitation. To what, exactly?

Daring to peek at Grant, she realized he was smiling at her, one side of his mouth dimpling up in a charming expression. "You never cease to surprise me." He picked her hand up, bringing it to his lips. She froze, hardly daring to breathe as he skimmed from the back of her hand to her wrist, leaving a trail of goosebumps.

"You know how to inspire me just as well as you know how to put me in my place." He placed another searing kiss on her racing pulse. "And I like how passionate you are about this town, how you're not afraid to love it with everything you've got." He placed one last kiss into the center of her palm before he released her hand.

He tilted forward and rumbled into her ear, sending electric shocks down into her core. "Did that answer your question?" The scent of his orange blossom and sandalwood cologne washed over her, obliterating any sensible response she could form.

Chapter 14

Breathless, she nodded. With a chuckle, he cleared his throat. "Well then, let's get to work on that form, shall we?" As he turned and leaned over the table, his shoulders flexing under his shirt, Ellie tried to shake herself out of her daze.

She needed to focus, but one look at his sculpted back told her that would be impossible. With a sigh, she bent over her notes pretending to concentrate. This crush was beginning to get out of hand.

* * *

Morning broke over the square in a burst of honeyed light and clouds swinging along on a crisp breeze. Grateful for the break from the heat, Grant rolled up his sleeves and turned his face to the sky, drinking in the clear day.

"I don't think I've seen you this relaxed... ever." Ellie studied him, head tilted to one side, a twinkle in her gorgeous eyes.

He leaned against her truck and tried to feign nonchalance. "Just enjoying a beautiful day with a beautiful woman."

She sputtered, cheeks coloring. "Could you be cheesier?"

He laughed, "Gotta give me points for trying."

Plopping a stack of flyers in his hands, she wagged a finger at him. "I'll give you points when we've got these filled out. Now march!"

With a cheerful shrug, he obeyed, heading towards the brick facades. As he studied the peeling paint and faded canvas overhangs, he hoped this was the turning point where they convinced people to begin seeing their town as worth investing in.

"You know, Mayor Patty asked me about the old railroad the

other day."

"Hmmm? What about?" Ellie straightened the flyers in her hands, working them into her clipboard.

"She wants to 'do something' with it." He watched her face for a reaction, and she frowned, pausing on the sidewalk.

"Do something? Did she specify?"

"Not really—just that she wants something creative."

With an eye roll, Ellie began walking again. "Just like Patty. Asking for the moon, but she really wants the stars." She opened the door of Stacy's Salon. "We should just pull up the old tracks and sell them for scrap and turn it into a nature preserve."

Grant chuckled. "I was thinking something a little more involved." Stacy eyed them over the counter as she arranged bottles of polish. Two blue-haired ladies glanced at them from driers in the back then went back to their magazines. "Like a wildflower garden… or something."

"What are we talking about?" Stacy leaned on one elbow as they walked up, clearly itching for some gossip.

"Nothing terribly exciting." Ellie elbowed Grant. He grimaced; he knew to let her talk from now on. "Just having fun thinking about things the old railroad could be turned into. Dreamin' is all."

"An RC track." Stacy nodded decisively. "My son loves racing those things. Have 'em underfoot all the time. Would love for him to have a nice place to take them."

"Now that is an idea." Grant shot Ellie a look and tapped the counter. "If you've got a sec,' we'd love to pick your brain about some ideas we've been working on."

Looking between them skeptically, Stacy nodded slowly, and Ellie handed her a flyer. "You see, we'd love to support you

Chapter 14

any way we can. And we think a Chamber of Commerce is the way to go."

"What in tarnation is a Chamber of Commerce?" Stacy ran her thumb over her brightly polished nails as she studied the sheet, her face turning speculative. Spotting her opening, Ellie launched into the pitch. Five minutes later, Stacy was nodding enthusiastically, calling out to the ladies in the back and making Ellie repeat herself. Grant handed each of them flyers with a smile. He doubted they owned businesses, but the further they could get the word out, the better. And he knew not to underestimate the power of gossip.

"Where do I sign, doll?" Stacy wrote her name in big loops of blue felt pen and handed the sheet to Grant with a flourish. "Can't wait to see more of what you two do!" He stared in disbelief at the signed paper. It had been so easy. All they had to do was ask.

As they burst out onto the street, Ellie was exultant. "First signature. That went well, don't you think?" He stared off into the distance as she chattered.

"I've tried to talk to people about different efforts before, and they weren't interested. What's the difference now?" Grant looked at Stacy's writing, scrawled across the page.

Ellie touched his back, smoothing her hand across it. "Look at how we formed the questions. There's no jargon. No words to obscure what we want to do. Everything is formed as action items—not hypotheticals. It's all about how you frame it." She waved her arm. "Know your audience and you can speak with your audience."

He leaned into her. "I've been in this business for years, and every job teaches me something new." Kissing her cheek, he whispered, "Thank you."

With a blush, she slid her arm around his waist. "You're welcome." They lingered there a moment before she drew away. "Now, we haven't got all day and we do have a lot of spots to hit." Sliding her hand into his, she pulled him down the street. "C'mon."

They worked their way down the street from Stacy's Salon to Al's Diner. Grant watched in amazement as owner after owner melted under Ellie's smile and bubbly explanation of what a Chamber of Commerce could do to support their business, from marketing efforts to lobbying.

So many happily signed that they were interested and filled out the rest of the form, indicating that they were in support of many of Grant's ideas. The very ideas they'd scoffed at only days ago. With her at his side, they even turned their smiles on him, winking and shaking his hand. Even the ones who refused the form did so pleasantly. Every room Ellie walked into, people turned to her, their faces lighting up.

As they emerged from Uncle Ray's Gun & Tackle with another completed form, Grant stared at Ellie in amazement. "How do you do that?"

She tossed her head back, laughing. "Talk to people?"

"Make them like you."

Looking thoughtful, she shook her head. "It's not about making them like me. There's no trick." She nodded her head at the street. "All of these people I've known for years. I know their stories. Heck, I'm in half of them. And the ones I'm not in, I listen to. I ask about their families and their pets. I reminisce about those who've passed on."

Her face turned wistful. "There's no magic. Only love."

He considered. If love was the key to Midnight Bluff, then it was no wonder he had stumbled so spectacularly

Chapter 14

here. He'd approached everything as a cut-and-dry business arrangement.

"Ok." He nodded. "Time to do things your way then."

"What do you mean?" A smile hitched up one side of her mouth.

He threw his arms wide, gesturing at the town. "It's time to 'love' Midnight Bluff!"

She guffawed, one hand over her mouth, as he grinned at her. He loved the lilting sound of her laugh. What he wouldn't do to hear it all the time.

Forcing a serious look onto her face, she nodded. "Ok, padawan, it is time for your next challenge. Come with me."

"What are we doing?"

She smiled at him mischievously as she put their flyers away into her backpack. "Seizing the moment."

* * *

"Nope. Nuh-uh. You're out of your mind." Grant froze on the sidewalk as he spotted the store they were headed toward.

Ellie rolled her eyes, grabbed his wrist, and pulled. "I thought you said you were ready to love Midnight Bluff."

"There is no way on God's green earth Herb is going to sign one of these. Not even after cleaning his lot." Grant remained planted on the sidewalk. Huffing, Ellie changed tactics and positions, shoving her shoulder into his solar plexus to get him to budge. With an *oof*, he began stumbling down the walk toward the Hardware Store.

"Of course, he won't if you never ask," she gasped as she kept shoving him. "But we're not asking him to sign a form."

Taken For Granted

"We're not?" Surprised, Grant stopped fighting her, and she smashed into him, colliding with his chest. His broad, rippling chest that was heaving from grappling with her. For a split second, she heard his heart thudding wildly against her ear, before she scrambled upright, straightening her backpack.

"Nope." She opened the door and ushered Grant inside as he continued to look at her skeptically. With her back firmly planted against the door, she allowed herself to grin. "We're asking him to lobby to change the zoning codes for downtown to mixed-use with the council." Grant stared at her aghast.

Behind him, Herb's deep, rumbling voice piped. "Are you now? And why, exactly, would I do that?" Grant grimaced, a comically exaggerated wince crossing his face.

Mouthing, *I'm going to kill you*, he turned to face Herb. Crossing her arms, Ellie watched from the door as the two men stared each other down. The staring match was getting ridiculous. Ellie breezed past them down the aisle, forcing them to break the silly contest off.

"Herb, don't you want to say something to Grant?" She looked at him meaningfully then out the window. Scratching at the back of his neck, Herb cleared his throat.

"Guess I owe you some thanks, for uh, clearing things up a bit."

Grant shrugged, arms crossed. "Don't mention it."

Men. When they had to deal with something difficult, they turned into Neanderthals. "Oh, I think you did him a big favor considering he was about to get fined, again, by the town for not upkeeping his property."

Herb shot her a glare. "Ellie!"

She shrugged. "If you kept the place up like you should, wouldn't be a problem, would it?" Grant was looking at her

Chapter 14

perplexed as well. She was being much more antagonistic with Herb than she had been with anyone else. Winking at him, she hopped up onto the counter, swinging her feet back and forth.

"So, Herb, as thanks for saving your tush, I think you should hear Grant out since he has a plan that could make you a lot of money. If..." She drew the word out with a lilting drawl. "... You're not too lazy to follow through with it." This was the kid who'd slept through all their classes in high school and made Bs when he could have been valedictorian.

Herb narrowed his eyes at her and crossed his arms. "Some of us have grown up, El."

"Mhmm. And some of us have yet to see proof of it." She waved an arm for Grant to take the lead as Herb raised his hands and dropped them in frustration.

Swallowing, Grant glanced between her and Herb. He raised his hands placatingly. "Look Herb, I'm not trying to step in your business."

"Nah. Go ahead." Herb hopped up onto the counter and sat next to Ellie, elbowing her. "Since apparently, my business is up for public discussion anyway."

Grant, scratching his chin, nodded slowly. "Most of the stores on Main Street were built in the late 1800s, early 1900s with two stories, right?"

Herb nodded. "Right. Office spaces. Apartments. Most of them are defunct now or used for storage, if the building isn't completely hollowed out."

"What if those upper floors were made into loft-style apartments? So, people could live where they work. Cuts down on urban sprawl. Makes a highly walkable area. Keeps a spending population highly concentrated and creates an invested community."

Herb nodded slowly. "I see what you're saying." He held up a finger. "But this area is zoned commercial only. Not residential. I mean, I can see getting storefronts rebuilt; that's just loans or business partners. But we can't just go building lofts no one can live in."

Ellie leaned an elbow on his shoulder, grinning. "Just wait for it."

"That's where you come in." Grant stood up straighter. "We need someone on the council to push for rezoning to mixed-use. Someone who believes that Main Street can become the heart of Midnight Bluff once again. All it takes is one council vote."

Herb shook his head. "And why would I stick my neck out like that? I've spent years building up trust with everyone in town to even be on the council."

Grant pointed out the window. "Because I believe you can see what this place can be with even a little bit of... of gumption." He took a breath. "Because lofts would mean steady rental income not just for you, but for all the other business owners in the area. And because the more people who can live in Midnight Bluff, the more taxpayer base you'll have to support the town and do all the things you've never been able to do before." He spread his hands. "Midnight Bluff deserves to be more than an afterthought. It deserves to be a home that people are proud of."

Warmth spread through Ellie as he spoke. He saw Midnight Bluff as she saw it. Not as an armpit of the Delta, but as a place full of caring, wonderful people who deserved so much more than life had handed them. The thought made her want to hug him and never let go.

Herb rubbed a hand over his mouth. "All right. But if I do

Chapter 14

this, I want your word that you'll give us more than some dang website and a few murals in this fancy plan of yours. I'm tired of hearing about non-fading paint."

"Done and done." Grant nodded at Ellie. "Want to show him the flyer?"

As they bent over the form with Herb, Ellie reached around and squeezed Grant's hand. Over the top of Herb's bent head. She mouthed, *I told you so*. Grant just rolled his eyes at her.

Chapter 15

Swerving to miss another pothole, Grant careened down Main Street. His commute would be so much shorter if these roads were...

He took a deep breath and blew it out of his nose. An infrastructure improvement plan was part of the overall proposal they were reviewing with Mayor Patty and the council today. Midnight Bluff's... crumbly... nature was one of the reasons Cress had called him after all. With a screech, he pulled up outside of the courthouse.

As he struggled into his suit jacket, his pocket let out a wild cacophony of EDM music. Only one person in his contacts list got such a vile ringtone.

"Hey, Todd!" He rammed his arm into his sleeve as he slung his briefcase around his shoulder so hard it swung around and dangled from his neck, choking him.

"Hey, man! Listen, the partners and I were looking at your file last night—" Grant's brain filled with white noise as he slapped at the briefcase. He'd been part of too many of those

Chapter 15

meetings, grimly studying the bylines of a colleague's career. Usually, at Todd's insistence.

Looking at someone's file only meant one thing: immediate termination. Todd's voice clicked on, "And up until Vermont, you've had an impressive track record. Things have washed out again in Mississippi, but I managed to convince them to give you one more chance. *If* you can cinch this deal and be out of there in two weeks." Todd was full of such bull. With a shake of his head, Grant knew he wouldn't get a second chance; whatever partner had saved his hide this time wouldn't want to stir up more drama. He had to politic this one out himself.

Face tingling as if he'd run through cobwebs, Grant answered, his voice even despite the trembling in his hands. "I'm about to walk into a council meeting now. Whole new proposal. They're going to love it." He swallowed against the tightness in his throat. "We have the perfect connections to get all the grants funded and other developments rolling. Should take minimal intervention once it's rolling."

A bang resounded over the line, the sound of a palm on a desk. A couple of beats later, Todd whooped, the sound loud and hollow. "That's what I wanted to hear. I knew you'd figure it out." It was Ellie who had given him the ideas, but before Grant could explain, Todd dropped his voice, suddenly intense.

"Listen, listen. You pull this off, and I'll make sure you get a sweet gig for your next project. None of these little no-name no-wheres. Something with real meat on it." Chuckling, Todd added, "This time next month, you could be looking back at this as the project that changed your career."

Nodding at the sky, Grant cleared his throat. "You can count on me." A project in a real city with resources to pull from? Maybe a downtown area to renew or a former industrial district that needed a new purpose. A developer's dream.

"Good. Now. Go get it done. Whatever it takes."

As Grant hung up, he pinched the bridge of his nose, his chest constricting with stress. If this vote didn't go well, he'd be out of a job and stuck in the middle of...

Forcing a deep breath, he released the tension bundling his shoulders and straightened his tie. He could only focus on one problem at a time. And the problem right now was this meeting.

His job was well and truly out of his hands. But this meeting he could still do something about. As he hesitated on the sidewalk, his eyes fell on the Loveless Bakery and Ellie's words rang in his ears: "Sometimes, you just need a little sugar to sweeten the deal." With a grin, he jogged across the square.

* * *

Ellie jogged her knee up and down nervously as she waited on the bench in the courthouse hall. She shouldn't have had that second coffee. And where was Grant? Glancing at the clock down the hall didn't help; the minute hand hadn't budged since she'd last looked at it, exactly thirty seconds ago.

Finally, the clack of dress shoes on tile met her ears, and she sprang up. Grant rounded the corner, a pastry box in his hand. He paused as she stared at him, hands on her hips and eyes wide. His Adam's apple bobbed once in his throat before he quipped, "Someone's been hitting the coffee pot a little too hard this morning." The dimple was back in full force this morning, and her heart somersaulted traitorously at the sight.

Chapter 15

She felt her cheeks shift upward and willed herself to relax into professional nonchalance. "And you've been spit shining your shoes since sunrise." She pointed at the overly polished leather objects adorning his feet. She'd opted for her trusty, and scuffed, leather work boots as usual—even if she'd cleaned them and thrown on a nice linen blouse instead of her usual plaid shirt.

"Guilty as charged." He shrugged. "I find it soothing." Raising an eyebrow, he chuckled. "If the only thing I can control about a situation is my appearance, I'll take it."

Ellie couldn't help herself. "What if it rains?"

"Bite your tongue!"

She smirked at his appalled face. "You can't control everything."

"Especially not a smart-aleck like you. Aren't you supposed to be backing me up today?"

Hoisting her backpack to her shoulder, she grinned. "That's what I'm here for. A huge boost of confidence right when you need it."

As he opened Mayor Patty's door for her, he leaned over and whispered in her ear, "Go, team!"

An embarrassingly high-pitched giggle escaped her lips just as she stepped through the door. Both Mayor Patty and Mrs. Emma Jean Hicks, the high school principal, looked up at her, eyes rounded in surprise. Ellie froze, Grant trapped in the doorway behind her.

With a creak, the door swung to, hitting Grant's backside, and slamming him into her. They stumbled into the room, Grant instinctively reaching out and grabbing her waist to hold her upright as she tripped over a chair.

As they extricated themselves, Mrs. Hicks stood upright,

mouth quirked to the side. Mayor Patty folded her hands on top of an open binder.

Nervously, Ellie brushed her hair behind her ears and swatted Grant's hands away from her waist. Her eyes darted to Mrs. Hicks who stood studying her, mouth pressed into a thin line and shoulders… shaking? Yep, they were being laughed at.

Great way to start this meeting. Mayor Patty's eyes twinkled as she flipped the binder closed and handed it to Mrs. Hicks.

"Your notes are thorough as always, Emma Jean. I'm sure the school board is going to be just as devastated as I am to see you leave in May." Patty winked at her. "Now if you'll excuse me, I have some yahoos of my own to see to."

Mrs. Hicks smiled at her. "Don't let them run wild with our town now!" She waved at Patty as she scooted around Ellie and Grant, shooting a mock stern look at Ellie. "You keep him in line now, you hear?"

Ellie nodded mutely. Before she sashayed out the door, she turned back to Mayor Patty, "You will be at my retirement party, right dear?"

Glancing up, Patty smiled, her eyes indulgent. "Wouldn't miss it for the world."

With a nod, Mrs. Hicks flicked out the door. "Sorry about that. Trying to find a replacement for her is going to be dang near impossible, but she's already put off her retirement near on five years now." Mayor Patty rubbed at her temple and blew out a breath, rattling the papers on her desk. She looked up at Ellie and Grant.

"All right. I believe I got the gist of everything in the file you sent me last night, Grant, so we don't need to hold everyone else up reviewing anything. I've requested that today's meeting

Chapter 15

be closed to the public, so that we don't get bogged down in debate. The finer points of your proposal can be discussed ad nauseum later—I just want to know the council is on board today. Does that work for you?"

Grant nodded. "Perfect. Keeps things simple."

"Let's get started then." She grinned at them, rising and waving them to follow her. "Before y'all manage to knock something over."

With a smile, he stepped forward and handed Mayor Patty the pastry box. "For you."

Genuine surprise lit up Mayor Patty's face as she flipped open the lid. The smell of vanilla, sugar, and lemon filled the room. Delighted, Patty pressed a hand to her chest. "Why, Grant, this is so thoughtful of you. Lemon squares!" Ellie had to give him props; he was a fast learner. Bringing the pastries was a good move.

He shrugged, looking as pleased as a cat that just ate the canary. "Someone might have mentioned they're your favorite." With a wink at Ellie, he added, "Thought you might like them."

"Well, it's plenty to share, so I'm sure it will perk everyone right up." Sure enough, as they filed into the meeting hall, Ellie grinned as she watched the council member's eyes zero in on the pastry box.

Mayor Patty handed the box back to Grant with a wink. "I'll let you do the honors."

As he handed out lemon squares on pieces of paper towel scrounged from a sideboard, Ellie quickly passed out folders of their new proposal.

Mayor Patty bit into her lemon square with a delighted mmm. "These must be your favorite, Grant." She winked at Ellie as she took another bite.

Confused, Grant asked, "Why's that?"

"Because they're so sweet and sour, just like you!"

As guffaws broke out around the room, Ellie elbowed Grant in the ribs playfully. "You got me there, Patty." He took a big bite of his own lemon square, grinning.

With the last folder passed out, she and Grant slipped into their seats, holding their breath as the council members munched and read. Herb glanced up, winking at them, then bent his head back over his folder.

Fidgeting, Grant leaned toward her. "It's been a while since I've seen them take notes." Ellie raised an eyebrow. Betty Coleman scrawled across her pages, while Bo McBride circled and starred his.

"Really?" She'd attended enough open council meetings to have seen how ardently the council members marked their notes. It was telling they'd tuned out Grant to the point of even foregoing doodling.

Mayor Patty absently flipped through her folder. After a few minutes of silent reading, she sat forward. "Alright. I believe we've had time to review." Upon receiving nods all around, she proceeded.

She sat up straight, setting aside her treat and steepling her fingers. In a formal voice, much more serious than her greeting, she opened. "I'll cut straight to the chase, Mr. Emberson. What makes you think that this proposal is so different from your other ones?"

Ellie sucked in a breath, holding it anxiously as Grant fidgeted in his seat. He leaned forward, resting his elbows on his knees. She heard the inhale before he answered, "I listened." He gestured to Ellie, and she felt a flush from her

Chapter 15

navel up to her cheeks as Patty glanced at her appreciatively. "I listened to someone who is part of and deeply cares about this community. Who knows what the members want and what they need. And together, we've incorporated those items into a sensible plan of action that has tangible results. Some of them, nearly immediate. Some take time and patience."

He clasped his hands. "This is more than what you asked me for. You wanted something to spruce up the town right now. But this is a long-term plan with long-term results. Execute it right and you'll be setting up Midnight Bluff for decades of success."

Across from them, Ellie saw Bo McBride nod slightly. Two stood in their corner then. That just left Betty Coleman as the unknown factor. And since Mayor Patty couldn't vote, they needed a unanimous decision today to adopt the plan.

Betty sat back in her chair. "I'll admit this looks great on paper. It hits a lot of the points we want and some we didn't even know we needed." She crossed her arms. "But this is a lot of work. And don't think we've missed the price tag. Renewzit is a Wisconsin-based company. How can you assure us that you will see this through here in Mississippi?"

Ellie tried not to flinch. Betty was voicing some of her own doubts. Knowing that Grant would be leaving once the first few steps were in place... she clenched her fists in her lap.

But Grant was already nodding. "I understand your concerns. That's why the plans we develop rely on community involvement, local developers, and a variety of federal and state grant funding as well as private investments."

He rubbed a hand over his mouth. "To be frank, we're consultants and middlemen." He tapped the proposal. "There is nothing in here that you couldn't do for yourselves with a lot of research and hard work. But Midnight Bluff is short on time and resources."

"So, what makes Renewzit a good partner is that we cut through all the data, we reduce learning time, and we help you through the decision-making process. When you're ready to start, we already have the contacts and the know-how to get your projects up and running sooner and better. By having such a high level of community involvement from the start, we have a track record of continuous growth in the towns and cities we partner with." He spread his hands. "This is a lot of words for: we help shape your future, but you're the ones who ultimately build it."

Pursing her lips, Betty nodded. Ellie jogged her knee up and down, willing someone to speak.

"Well, that was well-said." Mayor Patty tapped her fingers on the arm of her chair. "Anyone else have questions before we move to vote?"

The air conditioner kicked on with a rusty wheeze in the silence. "Then let's not dawdle. We have other business to address. Show of hands. All those in favor."

With a smile, Bo raised his hand. "You did good, son. Ellie."

Cutting his eyes at Betty, Herb raised his hand. After a second's hesitation, Betty raised her hand as well, frowning slightly. Jubilation shot through Ellie as Grant murmured, "Thank God." He looked up at Betty and said, "I'm happy to speak further when it's convenient for you." Her eyes widening in surprise, she bobbed her head.

"Accepted." Mayor Patty nodded, a satisfied gleam in her eye. "This is a provisional measure accepting the Renewzit proposal. At a later date, we will have a public hearing to address any concerns, but for now, we will consider ourselves

Chapter 15

be in a verbal agreement with Renewzit and authorize them to draft a contract."

The rest of the meeting passed in a haze, with Herb barely getting a murmur of dissent when he proposed a measure to rezone Main Street. They scheduled the public hearing for the next open meeting without any fanfare. An hour later as the council members filed out, Ellie watched as they each shook Grant's hand. Herb slung an arm around Ellie's shoulder. "Always knew you'd get into politics one way or the other."

She made a face at him. "Politics?"

He jerked a thumb at Grant as he stood talking with Betty. "Y'all are pretty much a package deal now. Politics come with the territory."

Her eyes widened with shock. "We're not…"

Herb chuckled. "Sure looks that way." But Grant was walking their way, and Ellie just sputtered in protest, face red. With a grin, Herb shook his hand and strode off.

"What was that about?" Grant asked, looking confused.

"Just congratulating me… us." No way on God's green earth was she about to tell him what Herb had just said.

A hug enveloped them from behind. Mayor Patty beamed up at them, her dark eyes shining. "Come! Let's celebrate." She bustled them out of the courthouse and down the street. The nostalgic smell of bourbon and cigarettes washed over them as she ushered them into the Southern Comfort Bar, mostly deserted on a late Tuesday morning.

"Lester!" With a wave, Mayor Patty signaled for drinks for everyone, and droopy-looking Lester slid glasses of bourbon down the bar to them as they hopped onto stools.

"Oh, you two." Mayor Patty still clutched the folder in her hands. "I love everything you've done in this." She swiped at her eyes. "After the other church closed two years ago, I was this close to giving up." She held up her fingers, only a pinch apart. "But this gives me hope that…" She glanced out the window. "…that I haven't had in a long time." She placed a hand on Grant's shoulders. "If no one else says it, thank you. Thank you for believing in this town."

She reached over and grabbed Ellie's hand. "And thank you for helping us. I know how much time this has taken away from your business. You've always come through even when no one else sees it." A lump rose in Ellie's throat. She twisted her hands together as tears stung her eyes. This was why she worked so hard—to make sure her town would never have to struggle like this again.

Patty let go of them with one last little pat and settled back in her seat. She cleared her throat. With a twinkle in her eye, she pointed between, "Y'all's working relationship has been so good. I have to say I'm impressed. The quality of work you've come up with in just a few days… Your partnership has been very fruitful." A slow grin spread across her face as she leaned back in her chair. "I can't wait to see what else is born out of it."

A furious blush heated Ellie's face. Grant squirmed in his seat and tugged at the knot of his tie. "Yes, well. Having such an intelligent co-worker makes the work a lot more enjoyable." He coughed.

Patty's grin widened, but she held up her hands, dropping the subject. "I do have a favor to ask. As someone who greatly enjoys our Bingo Hall, I'm not knocking it. But it does concern me that it and Ouida's Needle Shop are the two busiest places in Midnight Bluff. And the average age of the attendees is sixty-seven." She took a sip of her bourbon. "We need some

Chapter 15

young blood back in this town—we're dying out faster than we can breed 'em."

Grant spluttered on his drink, and Ellie thumped his back laughing. As she picked up her glass of bourbon and ice, contentment welled up in her, happy to be sitting here with good drinks and good friends.

Swinging her legs around to face them, Patty pulled a blank sheet from her folder. "So, one area that I'd like to see strengthened in the contract, if possible, is how to draw in younger small business owners and single entrepreneurs. What incentives, what infrastructure, what amenities—what specifically do we need to develop to draw them here?" She scrawled notes across a loose sheet of paper and slid it to them. Grant picked it up, already nodding, his eyes focused on the sheet.

Ellie's mind was a complete blank. Young people? Young people didn't come to Midnight Bluff. They left. In droves. Right after high school. There wasn't anything here for them. She stared in consternation at Mayor Patty.

"But we don't have anything to offer them! There's no start-up culture here. No investors. We don't even have our own bank or a full post office. Where would they get start-up capital?"

As she spoke, a dreamy smile spread across Patty's face. She tapped her fingers on the bar. "Now that's an idea." Snapping her fingers, she then patted Ellie's leg. "I see why he likes having you around."

"I've got some strings to pull. Some old friends of mine in the finance and development industries." She hopped off her stool—abandoning her drink. Ellie was not about to leave good bourbon behind. With regret, she tossed the rest of it back like a shot as Mayor Patty continued. "I'll invite them up here for one of y'all's presentations next week… And if they like what they see, I'll ask them to invest in Midnight Bluff!" She tapped the side of her nose. "Ooh! I like this idea!"

As they slipped back out into the sunshine, Ellie's mind spun with this turn of events—from near calamity to pitching investors. Grant's head must be spinning.

But no, he stood next to her with a smile on his face, shaking Patty's hand. Hugging Ellie, Patty swept away back to the courthouse.

And then Grant and Ellie were alone on the sidewalk outside Southern Comfort, morning sun washing over them.

Ellie looked up at Grant. "Did that just happen?"

With a whoop, Grant hugged her and spun her around on the sidewalk, all the answer she needed.

If this was what happiness was made of, she would take a double helping, please. As her feet finally touched earth again, his hands lingering on her waist, she looked up into his face. His eyes glowed with victory, and he leaned over her smiling, his bangs, for once wild and tumbled into his eyes.

Giggling, she reached up to brush them aside. An assurance that she could conquer anything with him by her side washed over her, enveloping her in a peaceful cocoon.

In the next moment, a certainty that he'd never settle for a tiny town and a country hick like her crashed right through the bliss that this morning's success had brought. Grant was brilliant. And no doubt, some boss back in the big city would swoop him up into a sparkling high rise and on up the career ladder. Trying not to let her chin wobble, she gently pushed his arms away and stepped back.

Their relationship—working and otherwise—had an expi-

Chapter 15

ration date stamped on it. And it was time to stop letting her crush on her co-worker run away from her. For both their sakes.

* * *

Ellie's face dimmed and her mouth pursed up as she suddenly stepped away. Grant froze, wondering if he'd gone too far in his jubilation over their win with Mayor Patty. Brainstorming ideas that appealed to young entrepreneurs? He was the man for that.

But as Ellie drew away from him, leaving the space between them cold and tense, he shook with doubt. He didn't want to lose the one real friend he had here. As her eyes darted towards the courthouse again and again, it dawned on him.

He stepped forward, taking her hand. She cringed and tried to pull away. He let her, even though everything in him screamed to cling tight. "Ellie, what Mayor Patty said… are you all right?"

Her eyes darted back to him, fastening on his face. "What do you mean? She loved the proposal."

Awkwardly, he flopped an arm between them. "I meant about you and me. What she implied…" He shoved his hands in his pockets as Ellie winced. "Are you still ok working with me after that?" He rushed to add, "Because obviously, I find you attractive," He wanted to kick himself as her eyebrows shot up. "You're very… and if things were different… But if any of this is too…" Her eyebrows shot up more, and her mouth twisted to the side. "…. What I mean is: I'd love to keep working with you, but if you feel uncomfortable at all,

I get it, and I respect that." He stuttered off into silence after the world's cringiest attempt at a "define the relationship" talk ever.

Ellie blew some air out between her lips, letting them vibrate in an adorably frustrated way. She looked down the street for a moment, and Grant squirmed in the silence. "I'm… ok. Patty's always been one for meddling." She crossed her arms and hunched her shoulders. "It's not that big of a deal. We're cool."

A light flicked on inside of him at the prospect of more time together. "All right!" He bounced on the balls of his feet. "Let's get to work, then!"

Shaking her head, Ellie pulled out her phone. "I have a signing to get to. It'll have to be this afternoon." She took a few steps backward, already turning away, eyes focused on her phone as she typed a message in. Something stretched taut in Grant's chest.

"I'll come with you!" The words were out of his mouth before he'd realized.

She turned to look back at him, surprise etched on her face. "Why?"

He swallowed, churning for an explanation. "You've helped me, gotten a glimpse at what I do. I'd love to see a true real estate mogul at work." Miming punching her arm, he added, "Teach me some of that Southern charm."

Ellie chuckled, "Goofball. All right." But she spun back to him holding up a finger. "But no talking! Silent as the grave." She muttered. "I don't need my clients magically getting into a fistfight because of you."

With a grin, Grant saluted her. "Yes, ma'am."

"Now you're getting the idea. Manners!" She took off down the sidewalk, already dialing her phone. Behind her back,

Chapter 15

Grant fist pumped the sky, still riding the high of the morning's victory, then sprinted to catch up.

* * *

Another buzz lit up Grant's phone. His mother hadn't stopped texting him celebration gifs since he'd told her the news of the proposal's approval. While they weren't completely out of the woods yet, he had to smile as he saw a picture of a bottle of champagne spewing everywhere.

MOM: Go celebrate your success!

GRANT: We celebrated Southern style—with bourbon.

MOM: *emoji of an eyes wide face* Now that's the way to party.

MOM: Was the girl you mentioned with you?

GRANT: Moooom....

MOM: Omg, she was!

GRANT: Maybe

MOM: I hope it's going well between you two.

Grant: It is

MOM: *smiley face emoji*

With a smile, he put away his phone as they rattled over the cracked brick streets. Sneaking a look at Ellie, he saw a little smile floating on her lips. He stared back out the window. He couldn't wait to see what Midnight Bluff looked like when the streets were smooth and full of life once again, and all because of them.

Chapter 16

Grant sat silently in a corner watching an exhausting stack of paper move up and down the table. As pens scratched over the sheets, his head spun from the amount of paperwork passing back and forth. He'd never bought property before but signing an onerous lease for an apartment now seemed like a walk in the park compared to this. The endless stream of deeds and bills made him break out in a cold sweat. No wonder homeownership was so daunting to people.

In front of him, Ellie sat at the conference table, looking calm, even at peace, as she collected an ever-growing pile of documents. Glancing over her shoulder, she winked at Grant then turned back to her client, an older gentleman who'd come dressed in what Grant now recognized as the farmer's uniform around here: worn boots, long-sleeve work shirt, and fading jeans.

After what seemed like an eternity, everyone stood to their feet, shook hands, and moseyed out of the dim attorney's office.

Chapter 16

The mood lightened as soon as the paperwork disappeared, voices lifting and shoulders rolling back—even a friendly glance or two tossed Grant's direction. The farmers at the center of the day's exchange stood chatting like old friends in the parking lot as Grant and Ellie strolled to the car.

They sat for a moment in silence as Ellie kneaded at her shoulder. She rested her head on the steering wheel. "Thank God that's over." She flicked the ignition on. "Maybe now I can get my roof fixed." She bit her lip, wincing.

Glancing at her pinched face, Grant *hmmed* in his throat. He didn't want to embarrass her; he could tell from her clothes and backpack that money was tight. But as his momma always said, "You don't go poking into other people's business unless invited." He pointed back toward the building, giving her an out. "You were pretty impressive in there." With a grin, he added, "Must have been some deal y'all were working out, from the paperwork."

Her face melted into the most kissable smile, as his heart sped up, tripping over itself. "Oh, gosh. No!" She waved a hand in front of her face as she laughed. "Just a cash sale of a cow pasture."

He reared back laughing. "So, you're telling me—that was a simple closing?"

Tears leaked out the corner of her eyes as she nodded. Leaning forward, he brushed them away with his thumb as they continued to giggle. "I mean, there's still the property deed, and the bill of sale, and tax declarations—"

Cradling her cheek in his palm, he looked at her, every cell in him wanting to be closer. "That just makes you so much more impressive. Making every client feel so important." Silently, she licked her lips as she gazed up into his eyes, chest rising and falling.

Not giving himself time to think, he pressed his lips to hers, softly, so softly, breathing in the taste of sugar and coffee and a heady sweetness that was all her own. Warmth burst in his chest, sparking outward along his limbs in heady surges and pops. He could have stayed there forever kissing her. Except that he felt her breath hitch as she inhaled, then froze under his touch.

He pulled away. "I'm sorry... I thought..." He stared out the window towards Main Street feeling like an idiot. Why did he always leap too fast with these Southern women? Giving his heart where it wasn't wanted. The thought made his chest seize up.

Oh. Oh no. This was bad. He couldn't be... in love with Ellie Winters, could he? A surety crept over him. He was and he was well and truly screwed. There was no way a woman as amazing as she would go for a jerk like him. A jerk who couldn't even read the moment right.

A warm palm slid into his, squeezing his fingers and arresting his racing mind. Turning back to Ellie, he saw her staring at her lap. "It's ok. I... I'm glad you kissed me." She tucked her chin farther down. "I wanted to kiss you too."

Relief surged through him so powerfully it felt like a lightning bolt running down his spine. He pulled her to him and wrapped his arms around her as best he could in the cramped space. The feel of her small body curled against his was headier than any drink he'd ever had. He wanted to spend the rest of the day—the rest of his life—wrapped around her.

A thought jolted through his gut. Now that the council had accepted his proposal, it was only a matter of time until he'd be leaving Midnight Bluff— leaving her. Tightening his arms,

Chapter 16

he buried his nose in her neck. The timing of it all was unfair. What would he do without her by his side?

The ring of a cell phone made them both jump, chuckling nervously. Shooting him a shy glance, Ellie grabbed at her phone. Grant could barely make out the garble of a man's voice in the quiet of the car. She jotted down a few things and said goodbye.

Taking a deep breath, she turned to him, her face cool and blank. Resisting the urge to reach for her again, Grant smiled. "Another client, huh?"

Ellie nodded, her façade cracking just a sliver as she bit her lip. "Wanting to meet with me now." She nodded towards the square, a few blocks away. "You good to walk?"

Disappointment clapped down on his shoulders. "Yeah." He swung the door open and clambered out, sliding the strap of his briefcase over his shoulder. He guessed he could find somewhere other than the courthouse basement to work today. As he was about to close the door, Ellie called his name.

"Grant!" She leaned across the seat, peering up at him, face framed by her auburn waves and eyes intense. "I will see you later, right?"

A grin slowly stretched its way across his face. "Of course." He'd make sure of it now.

As the sound of her engine faded in the distance, he turned toward the square, throwing a cheerful wave at the farmers. It wasn't until he was sliding into the lone booth with a wall socket at Al's Diner that he realized that they had waved back at him.

Chapter 17

Twilight began to creep around the edges of Midnight Bluff, softening the buildings and smoothing away the chips and cracks into something from another era. Something soft and romantic.

Ellie shook her head to clear her imagination and stared into Al's Diner to where Grant sat hunched over his computer. Nerves fizzled in her stomach, bubbly and nauseating. She longed to just turn away and leave this mess behind her to deal with another day. But if she didn't go in now, she'd end up avoiding him for...

Yanking the door open, she strode in, tilting her chin up. Enough with this grade-school crush nonsense. They were adults. She could handle herself around him. Had to before this got any more out of hand. There couldn't be any more kissing sessions like earlier today.

No matter how much his kisses gave her tingles and sparks all over that lasted for hours. A grin tried to break across her face, and she forced it down. She had to be calm. Professional.

Chapter 17

Cold as the Winters of her name to do this.

As she slid into the booth across from him, his eyes lit up, that annoyingly cute dimple appearing in his cheek. Her stomach flipped traitorously, and she twisted her fingers together in her lap to keep them from shaking. Dang it.

"Hey, you." He sat back, running his hands through his disheveled hair. Loosening his tie, he grinned at her. "Been gone a while. Hope it went well."

She shrugged, her thoughts flicking with irritation to this latest time-suck of a showing. She'd prowled through every last inch of the catfish plant as the potential buyer asked promising, intelligent questions. Then, right as she was about to go in for the hard sell, they'd waved a hand, said it was no more than a "derelict," and traipsed off into the literal freaking sunset. Without so much as a thank you for her time.

"'Bout as well as anything has been going for this listing." She waved at Al Jr. who nodded at her. Within seconds Mira, her hair truly impressive in a twist out, the ends of her dark curls touched with red, appeared with a steaming cup of coffee. Nodding gratefully at Mira, Ellie took a long sip, delighting as the caffeine hit her bloodstream. "Just what I needed after this afternoon."

Grant studied, his fingertips reaching out to brush her wrist. "I'm sorry it didn't go the way you hoped."

"Very few things ever do." She sat back, withdrawing her hand and watching as disappointment flicked across his face. She crossed her arms, hugging herself, her heart rattling against her ribcage and demanding to take the reins. "But it's over now." He tilted his head and opened his mouth to ask her a question, but an urge to put this off rose in her, propelling her forward. She lunged across the table and spun his laptop toward her.

A colorful brochure filled the screen. As her eyes swept over it, Grant spoke. "I've been working on Mayor Patty's request." His breath was warm against her cheek, and she realized he'd leaned forward too. He nodded at the laptop.

"For young business owners." She scrolled the brochure, marveling at the detail. "You came up with all this in one afternoon?"

He blushed. "When I'm inspired, I work quick." He bobbed his head. "Besides, Renewzit has put similar programs in place in other cities." He pointed at sections on the screen. "The problem wasn't the ideas. It was scaling them down to be doable for a small town. Tax incentives. Business training and incubation."

He sat back and swiped at his eyes. Dark circles ringed them, and Ellie wondered when he last slept through the night. "These are services you typically find in a much larger city. It's easy to absorb the upfront costs there. We'll have to get creative until those things can be put in place here."

She looked through the brochure. "So, you're more focused on selling chamber services, the town's atmosphere, and the planned infrastructure upgrades." It was a smart plan, marketing what they had as they got it. Not overpromising.

He cocked a forefinger at her "Exactly! Start with the things we can upgrade pretty quick. Even amenities will be…"

A jingle from the front door caught her attention. Dr. Washburn strode in, looking aggravated. Belatedly, Ellie realized they were camped out in his booth. An idea struck her.

"Hold on one second!" She sprang up and moved toward the door. Grant looked over his shoulder.

Chapter 17

"Ellie!" he hissed at her, but she chugged on ahead.

"Dr. Washburn!" Dr. Washburn just scowled at her. "How are you? I didn't get to say goodbye before you scooted out the other day."

"And did your friend tell you why?" Dr. Washburn crossed his arms.

Ellie scratched her nose. He was in fine fiddle today. She glared at the back of Grant's head as he scooched low in the booth. "He did. And he wants to buy you some pancakes to say sorry for being such a wad about everything." Out of the corner of her eye, she saw Grant's shoulders shoot up to his ears. Good, he heard that.

The corner of Dr. Washburn's mouth twitched up. He considered for a second then nodded. "All right, then. But just because it's you asking."

They tromped over to the booth, and Ellie poked Grant's side to make him scoot over in the small space as Dr. Washburn slid in across from them. She'd forgotten how narrow these booths were. Grumbling, Grant put his computer and notes away.

An uncomfortable silence settled over them. Grant stared at his hand as he tapped the tabletop. Dr. Washburn watched the bustle of the kitchen, fascinated by whatever Al Jr. had working in the kitchen.

Rolling her eyes, Ellie jogged her knee up and down, waiting for one of them to speak. "Oh, dear God! Will one of you start? This is just silly." Why were men always so slow to admit what they'd done?

Grant cleared his throat. He glanced nervously at Ellie, and she nodded her head toward Dr. Washburn, not letting him off the hook. But Dr. Washburn beat him to it.

"Look, I shouldn't have gotten mad the way I did the other day. Contracts and things… well, you're not wrong to bring them up." He shifted in his seat. "It's your job after all." Fiddling with his watch, he continued as Ellie and Grant stared at him, surprised. "It's a touchy subject is all. Took me by surprise."

Grant stuttered. "I was out of line. I should have thought about what I was saying… how it would come across. I was there when Van—"

Waving a hand, Dr. Washburn cut him off. "Van was a real piece of work. How he managed to pull the wool over all our eyes is… It's not something I'm proud of." Ellie studied the grey frosting the dark hair at his temples, the crinkles at the corners of his eyes. Despite how gruff he seemed at first, all his patients adored him, and she'd never doubted that Dr. Washburn had a good heart buried under all the stubbornness.

With a shake of his head, Grant rejoined, "But he was your neighbor for nearly forty years. Of course, you trusted him. I'm sorry if I made you feel foolish for relying on someone you should have been able to." Ellie squeezed his arm, knowing that her words had gotten through to him.

Dr. Washburn looked up at Grant. "True." He looked back down at the table, working his jaw. "Anyhow, all that's past." He sniffed and stared at Grant. "And you've got some plan for the future, which is a darn sight better than all the wallowing we've been doing, missing the glory days." He nodded to himself. "Yep, a darn sight better."

* * *

Warmth flooded through Grant at Dr. Washburn's words as

Chapter 17

Ellie's hand wrapped around his bicep. Camaraderie. That was the feeling. He'd felt an inkling of it with Herb earlier and now again with Dr. Washburn and Ellie. He didn't even realize how much of a relief it was to have someone finally understand what he was trying to do.

Under the table, he squeezed Ellie's knee. Her shoulder brushed against his ribs. "Dr. Washburn..."

"Clay. You can call me Clay."

Grant swallowed. "Clay. Can I buy you some pancakes?"

The man smiled at him. "Thought you'd never ask!"

With a chuckle, Grant waved at Mira and ordered them each a stack of pancakes with a side of bacon and a pot of coffee for the table to share. Just as they were tucking into the food with little moans of pleasure, someone patted Ellie on the shoulder and she turned toward them, pulling away from him, leaving his side cold.

He glanced up, mouth full of pancake, and hunched backward. Cress and Jake stood there, smiling down at everyone. Couldn't he get any space from them?

"We just wanted to come over and say hi!" Cress' teeth flashed in the fluorescent light. Jake stared at Grant while he chewed.

Ellie gestured to the table, glancing between Grant and Jake. "We were just chowing down on some pancakes."

Dr. Washburn—Clay— added, "And talking over some bright idea to paint a sign on the side of my silo," as he winked at Grant.

"Oh! That's awesome. It would be so nice to have something bright and cheerful to welcome people. I love it." Cress grinned at Grant as he rammed another bite of pancakes into his mouth, wishing for this whole awkward exchange to be over. "That must have been your idea, Grant."

All he could do was nod, silently, cheeks full. Why did this town have to be so confoundedly small that he saw Cress everywhere he went? They were ok now and all, but it would be *delightful* to have some space.

"Yep, he's good with the ideas. Just not so much with the people." Jake smirked at him over Ellie's head as if reading his thoughts. Grant wondered if it would be juvenile to take one of his pancakes and fling it at him. Probably. Besides, he didn't want to tick Mira off. He liked Mira.

Swishing her hair over her shoulder, Ellie sniffed. "At least he has ideas." Grant eyed her, surprised by the sharpness of her voice. Grinning, Jake just shook his head and shot a look at Cress. Her grin widened.

"Well, it was good seeing you. We'll let y'all get back to your dinner." Cress wiggled her fingers at them, and then they were blessedly gone.

"Nice couple. Real nice." Clay looked at him and then Ellie as he slowly cut off another bite of his pancakes. He rolled the bite around in his mouth, staring at them, before he added, "And she made a good point about the mural. It would be cheerful."

Grant looked to Ellie for an indication of their next move; slowly she dipped her chin in a slight nod. Somehow, with her meddling, Cress had given them an opening to talk to Clay about the silo again. And he wasn't going to question a second chance. He patted Ellie's knee in acknowledgment.

"It would be cheerful," he agreed as he turned back to Clay. "The perfect way to show visitors just how vibrant Midnight Bluff is."

Chapter 18

Light pooled around their feet as they stepped out onto the sidewalk. As the older man stepped away, Grant waved at Dr. Washburn—Clay, eventually, he'd get his name straight—and turned to Ellie. She'd already turned to go, not a word said.

Her demeanor was so different from her ready opinion and trilling laugh of earlier that he wondered if their kiss had upset her. She'd been so standoffish when she'd come into the diner, but he'd set it down to nerves. During dinner, she'd been quiet, rarely chiming into the conversation.

Now, she wouldn't meet his eye.

Indecision hummed in his chest until he groaned in frustration, grumbling deep in his throat as he watched her fumbling in her purse for keys. Maybe she just needed a good night's sleep. She'd said she'd had a long afternoon with a frustrating client.

Still, he didn't want to part without at least acknowledging each other. Even if she'd changed her mind and just wanted to be colleagues, not saying anything at all felt… cold.

Grant took a step closer. "So, this listing you mentioned…"

Ellie looked up, arm buried in her bag and eyes watchful. "Yes?" The word fell flat, opening a deep chasm between them.

He sucked in a breath, as the hairs on the back of his neck pricked up. Lamplight caught her eyes, turning them deep and unreadable as pools of water. Everything in his body yearned to touch her, to stroke the lines of her face and coax her back to him. A silver fob appeared in her hand.

"I'd love to see it." The words leaped over his lips in one fevered rush.

The corner of her mouth ticked up. "There wouldn't be much to see." She gestured to the town around them. "In the dark."

Outside their pool of light, night clung to the town, thick and unctuous as soup. He could barely make out the twinkling lights of the Loveless Bakery from where they stood. Still, he grasped at any chance to stay with her.

"I'm sure we'll be able to see something with this." He held up the tiny little flashlight he kept clipped to his keychain. The light at its end let off a spark no bigger than a firefly.

A laugh barked out of Ellie as she shook her head. "C'mon then." She waved him on as she turned towards her truck at the edge of the circle of light. "I guess you won't be satisfied until I show you what you want."

"Persistence. That's how you win. With life and the ladies," he quipped as he hustled to keep up with her. She scowled at him, but her mouth twisted to the side, trying to hide a smile. He grinned as he slid into the passenger seat, and they took off down the dark street.

Chapter 18

* * *

Gravel crunched under the tires as they rolled down a bumpy road into the syrupy night. Ellie rubbed her nose. What was she doing taking Grant to this rundown plant? She should be keeping her distance, not spending more time alone with him in the dark.

He chuckled, the sound breathy and high-pitched in the small space. "Maybe I should have asked where we were going first. Are you sure you're not taking me out into the woods to murder me?"

As they rattled across the old railroad trestles, she glanced around. Oak trees dangled over the road, Spanish moss draping their limbs. Early evening mist gathered at the edge of the road which was quickly disintegrating into nothing more than a gravel track through the woods.

"Does look a bit spooky at night." They swung around a bend and her headlights cut across the chain-link of the fence surrounding the catfish plant. She pulled up to the gate and cut the engine. "But we're here." From the backseat, she fished up a big workman's flashlight that she kept for camping with Vada.

Grant peered through the gloom. "Is that..." He cracked the door and swung out. "This is the old plant. The one everyone keeps talking about." Turning around in a circle, he paused when he spotted the lights of the town twinkling through the trees.

Ellie grinned at his flummoxed look. "Yep. We're about half a mile away. Feels like forever with the woods in between though, doesn't it?" She punched her code into the lock on the gate and led him in. "Entrance is this way."

Graffiti in rainbow hues swirled up the sides of the corrugated metal building, depicting whimsical versions of animals, people, and huge letters. Grant paused, considering the colorful sprays, reaching out to brush a hand over the paint.

"I try to keep this place locked up, but with this much old chain link…" Ellie shrugged, heat washing over her face. Kids were forever coming up here and tagging the building. She'd done it herself once with Vada and Willow after a glass or two of wine too many at the bakery. It was tradition. But the curled lips and squinted eyes of her clients recently made it feel like it was something low. Something poor and trashy.

Grant shook his head. "It's so… creative. I wish more towns had places like this." He stepped back, eyes sweeping along the wall. "Where there's art, there's life." He turned to her, his words thrumming through her as his eyes locked with hers. "It's beautiful."

A cool breeze touched her face. Swallowing, she flicked her flashlight along the wall, searching. "My name's there." Surprise rippled over Grant's face as his eyebrows shot up. He stepped over to examine the signature in plain white spray paint.

"Is this Vada and Willow's too?"

"We were having a girls' night. This is one of the wildest things to do around here without going into Cleveland."

He grinned, his teeth white in the moonlight. "Look at you, partying it up." Stepping closer, his eyes swept over her, filled with a heat that left her feeling scorched and light-headed. How could he make her feel completely seen even in the dark?

She hunched her shoulders, wishing she'd worn more layers even though the evening was warm. "Yeah, well." Striding off,

Chapter 18

she grabbed the door at the entrance to the plant. "C'mon."

This was a bad idea.

A really bad idea in the dark.

Silently, Grant followed her. Inside the plant, the sounds of crickets and the night breeze fell away. They walked past the gutted reception area and pushed through the big double doors into the main floor of the plant.

Power had long been shut off to the facility, so Ellie held her flashlight up, letting the beam play across the machines and conveyor belts. Grant whistled, the sound echoing against the metal.

"What is all of this?"

She flicked the light around, showing him the different stations, rust slowly beginning to eat its way up the stainless steel in the un-airconditioned Mississippi humidity. "Over there is where the fish were cleaned and chilled." She turned to a row of conveyors with box-like sections running down the sides. "Another group of preppers would break down and clean the fillets some more over here then…" she followed the conveyor, "Send them to be packed on ice or individually quick frozen here." She pointed to huge machines covered in dust.

Grant followed her as she picked her way around a puddle of water on the floor. It looked like she was going to have to ask for a favor to get the roof covered again from another leak. "And back here, the fillets were sorted by weight, bagged, and boxed." She pointed out the stations quickly, before leading him to the ginormous walk-in freezer and refrigerators.

"And this is where they were stored before going directly to restaurants, grocery stores, or customers." With a wave, she pointed to the loading dock bays to the left at the very back.

Nodding to himself, Grant looked around, pressing a hand over his mouth. "This is a fantastic space. I wonder…" he trailed off.

Curious, she pressed him. "Do you think we could get it running again? Find a buyer for it?" He had studied the local economy; surely, he knew a trick to attract buyers that she didn't.

He grimaced and her heart sank. "I'm sorry. But from the little I've seen of this place, no. Not as it is. There are not enough ponds left in the area and this equipment is…"

Heaviness pressed on her shoulders. "Outdated and broken down."

"Yes." He shrugged. "I think the building is worth something. The equipment… I'm not so sure about." He took a breath. "But I'm no expert."

"You're right though." She swung the flashlight around. "All of my prospects for this listing have said the same. Basically."

Scraping a toe across the sealed concrete floor, he *hmmed* in his throat. "It's a shame though. This building could be amazing." He pointed back to where they'd entered. "It's got a great entrance, plenty of floor space." He circled his arm then pointed to the back. "Those could be private conference rooms or workshop spaces…" Pushing open a side door, he poked his head out into the loading dock. "And a great space for a patio or open-air workshop."

Ellie stared at him, completely lost. "What are you talking about?"

"A co-working space. And it could be dirt cheap in a place like this. If Herb does put in lofts above some of the storefronts along Main Street, it's even within walking—"

Alarmed, she held up her hands, cutting him off. "My client

Chapter 18

wants to sell this place as is. Not run some 'co-working' space. Besides, I thought you said only cities had the money to support business incubators?"

Shaking his head, he gestured again, windmilling his hand. "I'm not talking about a business incubator with grants and coaching and whatnot. I mean a co-working space, where people pay rent to have a guaranteed space to come work and have services like a receptionist, mail receiving, printing, a basic break room—stuff you would get at an office but wouldn't necessarily have at home." His voice went up in pitch, gathering steam. "It's great for entrepreneurs who need a mailing address that's not their house or want the camaraderie of an office environment. With the right set-up, it can be pretty affordable too."

Ellie's head began to buzz. It was an intriguing idea, but she had no idea if Mr. Stevens would go for it. She'd be risking a lot in bringing this idea to him. Possibly, her entire contract with him. If she ticked him off, it could cost her other big industrial clients in the future, and then her real estate business would be hamstrung.

But Grant was looking around, a gleam in his eye. "This space..." He strode away, waving his arms. "Is amazing. With minimal construction, you could have a ton of desks or tables. Some private spaces. Reception. And it's got enough land to it, that an easy expansion would be workshop space for creatives." He looked at her, chest rising and falling with excitement.

Slowly, she shook her head. "It's not that I don't think it's a good idea..." His face fell and her heart pinched in so quickly, it sent a jolt of pain through her chest. She held up her hands. "It's just that my client wants to sell this place part and parcel. He wants to be done with it."

She walked up to Grant and took his hand. "How would we find another buyer, in rural Mississippi, who'd want to take a place like this and turn it into what you're dreaming up?"

A sigh so soft she couldn't hear it washed over her cheeks as he leaned down to her. Gently, he touched his forehead to hers. "I know." He licked his lips slowly, the smooth skin glistening in the low light. "But this place could be so amazing if people would just take a chance on it that I—I just wish someone else could see it the way you and I do."

He shook his head back and forth, swaying her with him. "Just a crazy dream is all." He pressed a kiss to her forehead that left pinpricks of tears in her eyes, then stood up straight with a rueful smile. "Don't mind me. I'm always going to think big. Someone has to reel me in eventually, El."

With a sniff, he turned to walk back to the entrance, his shadow stretching out long in front of him in the glow of the flashlight.

"I'll ask him," Ellie whispered.

Grant turned on his heel. "What?"

"I'll ask him about… the co-working space." She tried to smile, but her lips quivered. So instead, she pressed them together. What in the world was she saying—risking—for a man who was going to leave her? But she'd already given her word now. "The worst he can do is say no, right?"

He tilted his head to the side, studying her. "Are you sure? I don't want to…"

She shook her head. "I'll ask." Hurrying past him, she held open the door. "Nothing ventured, nothing gained, right?"

He paused a second longer. A grin sweet as molasses eased across his face, light dashing off his teeth. "That's the spirit!" With that, he grabbed her hand and whirled her out into the

Chapter 18

night.

* * *

The keys were back in Ellie's hand. Pretending he didn't see them, Grant headed toward the railroad trestles that ran by the plant. Mayor Patty's request tickled at the back of his mind, a convenient excuse to keep Ellie close for another few minutes.

"Where are you going?" Her voice floated to him as he passed through the trees and hopped over the iron ties to stand on the old wooden planks, scrubby weeds and flowers poking up through them. A slight rustle sounded behind him and then the beam of her flashlight cut across the track.

"Oh." Gingerly, she picked her way over to him. "Thinking about what Patty said?"

He nodded, looking up and down the track. "Not sure what to make of a piece of land like this." Cupping her elbow, he began strolling down the old line. "It's so long and narrow, it wouldn't really make a good park." She remained quiet, her light fixed on the uneven ground. "I'm just not sure what to do with it."

"It runs through town." Her voice was barely a murmur.

He glanced at her. "Through town?"

She cut her eyes at him, still not really looking at him. "Mmhmm."

He turned in a slow circle, looking back the way they came then overhead. "It's so quiet out here. So peaceful. Does anyone else know about it?"

Ellie nodded. "Vada and I often bring the horses out here to ride. Makes a great trail."

He halted, rubbing at his mouth. "A trail." An idea sparked, lifting his chest. "Now that's an idea. A nature trail. There's a fantastic nature trail in New Albany that's built on top of an old rail line—I completely forgot about it because I thought it wasn't relevant. But this would be…"

She finished for him. "…an amazing amenity for the entire town. The surrounding area too."

Finally looking up at him, Ellie nodded. "An easy selling point for the council. And I'm sure there's grant money for that kind of thing." Grant nodded at her half-voiced question. She stared back at the plant, gnawing on her lip.

"It's the kind of thing that would be attractive to a young workforce looking for a healthy environment and would benefit everyone already here." He wasn't sure exactly how long they had left together, but he wanted to savor every minute with her. He hesitated, then wrapped her in a hug, resting his head on top of hers. "You inspire me so much, you know?"

She hiccupped a surprised laugh, but slid her arms wound around his waist. "I think you're selling yourself a little short."

Pulling back, he brushed a strand of hair from her face. "Maybe. But doesn't change the fact that you're amazing." She dropped her eyes and turned away as she crossed her arms over her chest.

"Grant, why did you come to Midnight Bluff? Was it… was it only for Cress?"

He blinked, the question rippling through him. Cress' face flashed through his mind, and he swallowed, his mouth suddenly sour. Midnight Bluff was so much more to him now than a collection of dilapidated buildings and a phone call from an ex.

Chapter 18

It was Herb's teasing every time he went to the hardware store for a screwdriver or plumbing tape. It was stacks of pancakes at Al's Diner and Mira knowing just how he wanted his coffee based on how his tie was tied. It was Willow's pastries and Mayor Patty's well-intentioned snooping and Ellie's laugh. The people were who made Midnight Bluff the place he'd come to love. His chest tightened at the thought of leaving.

But he couldn't lie to Ellie about why he came. "I came for Cress." In the near darkness, Ellie's shoulders hunched. He chafed her arms. "But I'm not who I was then. I've realized that love isn't something I can control or use to prop up my ego. It... sacrifices."

"And I stayed... I stayed because I love..." She stared up into his eyes. His mouth went dry as his heart thumped so violently against his ribs, he was afraid they would break. "I love small towns." His tongue felt leaden as he continued, clenching his fists.

If he was leaving, some truths couldn't be spoken between them. But he could give her another one. "I grew up in a small town, and it was the best childhood a kid could have. And I want to raise my own family in one someday. And if they keep dying out..." He let his voice trail off. "Well, I believe in Midnight Bluff. It reminds me of home."

Ellie's throat worked. He wanted desperately to reach for her, but something about the crystalline sheen of her eyes told him if he did, he might shatter the moment. "What about you? Why do you stay in Midnight Bluff? You could do so much in a big city."

She pushed her hair back, thinking. "This town—it's more my family than my own kin. The people of this town... They raised me; they still look after me. I just want to do something, anything, to keep them going." She whispered. "Education, jobs, stability— I want to give this town the chance for a future that my family never had."

Unable to help himself, he pulled her back to his chest and wrapped his arms around her. Whispering into her hair, he promised, "That's exactly what we're going to create together."

* * *

Ellie's armpits were sweating. Not a very elegant thing to be focused on right now, with her hand wrapped in Grant's, but it was true. Goosebumps rose on her arms as the trill and pitch of a whippoorwill's song whistled through the night air. She shivered at the plaintive sound, and Grant pulled her closer.

"There can't be anything worse in these woods than coyotes." He tried to laugh as he reassured her, mistaking her shiver for nerves.

She grinned at the thought of Grant, in his spiffy shoes, trying to fend off a coyote. "Oh, you'd be surprised." He looked at her askance, eyes wide in shock. "We've got bears, bobcats, and according to local legend at least, even a Bigfoot sighting or two." Elbowing him in the ribs, she smirked up at him.

He rubbed his side, grimacing. "Sharp words from someone who is snack-sized."

Rolling her eyes at him, she turned back to concentrating on picking her way through the woods to the truck. Her boots were great for tromping through fields and mud, but they weren't exactly meant for tromping through the woods. And the thought of a tumble into pitch-dark brush made her skip

Chapter 18

up the embankment quickly and back onto the gravel drive.

Grant huffed after her. "Trying to leave me behind to get eaten?"

"You're the one who took off through the woods on his own in the first place." She clicked off her flashlight and stared up overhead, drinking in the stars. As small as Midnight Bluff was, there was still enough glare from the rare streetlight to obscure this incredible view in town.

"Woah." Placing a hand on her waist and his chin on the top of her head, Grant took in the glimmering arch. "I don't think I've ever seen a sky this clear."

"Too much light pollution in the cities." She shook her head. "You know, if we're successful, this will be muddied too. I guess it's a small price to pay though for saving Midnight Bluff." The words stung despite the night breeze brushing over her skin.

Grant's arm slid further around her waist, and she let him pull her into the warm cradle of his body. "Then we'll have to make sure you never lose your night sky. Zoning codes and all that." In the distance, the whippoorwills sang to each other, a soft, lulling warble, a delicate call and response of love as he gazed into her eyes. Her knees trembled with the desperate urge to ask him to stay, to never leave her and this town.

A shooting star flashed overhead. She pointed. "Look!"

His eyes widened. "I haven't seen one of those since I was a little kid. What did you wish for?"

She swiped at his shoulder, trying to hide the tremor in her voice. "It doesn't work like that, silly."

"Well, I know what I wished for." Grinning, he leaned forward and, with firm lips, planted a kiss that scorched her down to her core. Heat blossomed in her stomach, and by the time he released her, her hands were curled into the fabric of his shirt, her chest rising and falling in quick breaths. "I always wish for more."

Chapter 19

Ellie stared at the phone in her hand, electricity running through her. The sound of Willow clattering a tray down onto the counter brought her back to herself. Mr. Stevens had agreed to the meeting. And he had agreed to see them in, she checked her watch, twenty-two minutes, no less. Grant stared at her expectantly over his coffee cup from his usual seat in the Loveless Bakery.

"What did he say?" He bit into a croissant as he set the cup down.

"He's on his way now. Wants us to meet him at the hardware store." She took a breath, forcing the air down to the bottom of her spasming lungs. "He'll be here in twenty minutes."

Crumbs flew across the table as Grant sputtered. "Now?!" He scrambled for paper and pens then threw the whole mess on the table in irritation. "How am I... What will... How am I supposed to put together a pitch that quick?"

He massaged his temples then scratched at the scruff on his chin. "I haven't even shaved today!" Ellie studied the dark circles rimming his eyes. It looked like he hadn't slept again. She slid her hands into his and gently pulled them away from his face.

"Hey." She tried to sound steadier than she felt. "All you have to do is tell him the same thing you told me last night. All I said is that we have an idea we want to float by him. You don't need an official spiel." Squeezing his hands, she smiled, pushing down the tremor of misgiving rippling through her belly. "Just be the smart, charming man you are. That's all."

He let out a breath, brushing his thumb across her knuckles. "Ok." He inhaled and closed his eyes. "Ok." When he opened them again, calm eased the lines of his face. "We've got this."

An easy assurance washed over her as she smiled for real. "Yeah. We've got this."

Willow whistled from the counter. "Oi! Love birds! You need to pack up and get going if you want to beat him over there."

"It's just across the square!" Ellie protested. But she stood anyway, abandoning her croissant with a bitter look, and slipped her notes into her backpack. She hustled after Grant out the front door. The sooner they got this over with the sooner she would know if she would be blocked from industrial real estate for good.

* * *

Mr. Stevens plodded up the aisle of Herb's hardware store, Ellie and Grant trailing after him. This wasn't the most unusual place Ellie had ever brokered a deal, but it was close. The winner was still a seedy strip club one of her clients

Chapter 19

had managed to find in the back of an old pharmacy. She'd managed to keep her cool and close the lucrative sale, but they had parted ways after that.

Poking at a steel part on the shelf, Mr. Stevens eyed Grant then Ellie, as Grant enthused first about the possibilities of the space in the plant, the potential for expansion, then the proposed nature trail. The older man's eyes narrowed as he screwed up his lips to spit into a Coke can he kept discreetly in his hand. After the introductions, he'd jerked his chin in a "let's get on with it" motion; Grant took it from there. The only sound Mr. Stevens had made since was an *mmhmm* or *uh-huh* at the appropriate points of Grant's speech.

Thankfully, Ellie had warned Grant of his taciturn nature on the short walk over. Mr. Stevens had the stature and disposition of a brick: short, sturdy, and silent. That didn't make him a stupid man, however. He had one of the sharpest minds she'd ever met. A mind sharp enough to not waste words on pointless things.

Ellie was sure that her fingernails were firmly embedded into the pads of her palms. Her eyes darted between the two: Grant waxing poetic about walking distance and Mr. Stevens eyeing a gearbox for his tractor.

As Mr. Stevens plucked it off the shelf, Herb appeared at Ellie's elbow, hands out for the part. Without a second glance, Mr. Stevens handed it to him and turned back to Grant, leaning an elbow on the shelf he'd just been looking at. Herb gave her a wide-eyed stare and walked past them down the row, clearly taking the long way back to the register, the better to eavesdrop on them.

Waving a hand, Mr. Stevens halted the flow of words. "Let me make sure I have the idea. You want me to gut my plant, renovate it, then become, essentially, a landlord to a bunch of young yahoos who may or may not have solid business plans?"

The knot in Ellie's stomach leaped up her throat as she watched Grant's shoulders tense. A second later they relaxed. "You're right. They may not have solid business plans. I can't make any guarantees on that. But these spaces are designed for single entrepreneurs and small businesses—they're hubs that drive economy. In any case, they will be paying customers for you, subject to your contract." Grant straightened his back.

An itch crept in between Ellie's shoulder blades. "Think of how a space like this gives a place for our young talent to grow into their businesses, instead of leaving for the cities. It could even give some who have left a reason to come back." Her thoughts flitted to Jackie, and Lorene, the sister she missed so terribly. The next aisle over, Herb shot her a warning look as he passed by.

Cupping his chin with forefinger and thumb, Mr. Stevens thought for a minute. "Hmm. It's an interesting idea." He lapsed into silence.

Interesting. The death knell of deals everywhere. Ellie licked her lips as she looked at the speckled linoleum, bracing herself. "I'm sorry, Mr. Stevens. We shouldn't have bothered—"

"Now hold up!" He held up a hand. "Don't go racing ahead of yourself. I said in'neresting, not stupid." His drawl came out thick as syrup and followed by a smile. He waved at them to follow him to the front where Herb busied himself bagging up Mr. Stevens' items and openly gawking at them.

"This is the most original idea I've heard around here in a while. I am a businessman. It…" He tapped his teeth together. "Behooves me to ask a few questions. Now, that trail idea…" He pointed at Grant. "Is a real nice touch. And if we can

Chapter 19

get someone in on some affordable lofts..." Winking at Herb, whose mouth gaped open, he turned back to Ellie. "It sounds like an all-around sound idea. If..." He held up a finger. "...you can get some of the mayor's fancy pants investors in on it. Yes, I already heard about them—don't bother protesting. But I do want to see some other people liking and backing this idea."

As Herb slid his debit card back to him, Mr. Stevens patted Ellie on the shoulder. "You did good, bringing this to me."

He picked his bag up off the counter and turned to shake Grant's hand. "I got to say, you surprised me. Pull out a few more ideas like that, and we just might want to keep you around after all."

Sunshine blinded Ellie as she watched him plod out the door, the bells tinkling dimly overhead. As the door swung back in place, Grant whooped, grabbed her by the waist, and spun her around, jolting her back into reality.

As he planted a kiss on her cheek, Herb leaned forward onto his elbows on the counter, clearing his throat. Eyebrows drawn together, he waved his hands in a spreading motion, "Care to explain what you just roped me into?"

She swallowed, tightening her grip on Grant's hand. And now the real convincing had to begin.

Chapter 20

A bulb overhead flickered, giving Grant a headache. He shoved the papers in front of him away, rubbing at his eyes. "I don't think I can stare at this a minute longer." A poke to his ribs made him look up. Ellie held a to-go box toward him.

"You need to eat." She stared down at her notes, scratching more annotations to the side, as she held out the container to him. He looked at it guiltily then the clock. They'd picked up lunch over an hour ago. Suddenly, his stomach gurgled in protest at the neglect.

"Thanks." He grabbed the box and attacked the fried catfish inside hungrily. Even cold, Al Jr.'s handiwork was still delicious. Absently, Grant wondered if he'd begin to get the characteristic potbelly of the Southern gentleman if he stuck around eating this kind of food. A smile spread across his face at the thought of strolling down the trail with Ellie, years from now, both a little soft around the middle...

Leaning over, he tapped her shoulder, "Hey, do you think,

Chapter 20

with the nature trail, we should have some benches at intervals along it?"

She threw down her pencil. "I don't know, Grant! Who's going to be paying for those imaginary benches? The hordes of imaginary people that are going to flock to the co-working space?"

He blinked as the catfish went dry in his mouth. She scowled at him then looked back at her notes, smoothing her hands over the pages as her lips worked.

Sitting the to-go box down, he wiped his hands on a flimsy paper napkin. "El." He tipped her chin up to meet his gaze. "What's going on?"

She shook her head and broke away. "Nothing. I'm fine." Tapping the paper, she fixed him with a stare. "The town just doesn't have the tax base to support this is all." He raised his eyebrows, incredulous, and she repeated, "I'm fine."

"I may be a complete dunce when it comes to women, but I'm pretty sure I can tell when the issue isn't really the issue." He sat back in his chair, crossing his arms. "And considering I just spent the last half hour compiling a list of possible grants to pay for the trail, I don't think money is the issue. So…"

Biting her lip, she twisted her hands in her lap. "It's nothing. I'm just being grumpy and selfish."

He laughed, the sound echoing out the door of the conference room and earning a scowl from Mr. Leonard as he passed by. "I really doubt that." He leaned forward, taking her hand. "And if you are, well, you probably have a good reason. Not all selfishness is bad. Sometimes, it just means you're trying to take care of yourself."

Ellie dipped her head, hair swinging forward to hide her face. "I lost the contract."

Taken For Granted

The clock ticked in the silence as Grant's brain ground the pieces into place. The catfish plant, Mr. Stevens, the co-working space. Since Ellie would no longer be selling the plant for him, she would no longer be earning the commission from the contract on the plant either.

His stomach twisted, hot and sharp, threatening to send the few bites of catfish he'd just gulped right back up. However unintentionally, he'd hurt her. He'd noticed the wear on her truck, the patches on her backpack. Heck, he'd even noticed how carefully she'd mended the seams of her clothes. And he hadn't thought anything of taking a payday away from her.

"I'm so sorry. I didn't think..." He blinked as his eyes misted. All the good he was trying to do, and he still bungled it this badly with the woman he loved. The thought made his breath hitch. A squeeze on his fingers brought him back down.

"It's ok." She looked up at him, her eyes swimming into focus. "I'll be alright."

"I'll make this right. I promise." His voice wavered. "We'll get so much business going in this town—you'll be selling houses and signing leases left and right. We'll never have to worry about money again."

"Grant, it's alright. Really. You don't have to make promises that might not..." She swallowed.

"But I want to take care of you." A flush rolled up her cheeks and she dipped her head further. "What can I do to help you now?" He pressed his knee to hers, trying to see her face.

"I've got... I've got people. I just need to ask for help." She finally looked up at him, her face smooth. The corner of her lip quirked up in a half-smile. "I'm fine. Really." A grin worked its way slowly across her face. "As long as it doesn't rain too hard." She turned back to the work on the table.

Chapter 20

"You need a roof?" His voice cracked in the most pre-pubescent way possible and her laughter finally peeled out.

"Yes. But it's not that bad yet. It can hold out a little longer while I call in some favors."

Grant sank his head into his hands, heat rising in his chest at the thought of a rainstorm popping up in this fickle Mississippi weather, water dripping on her while she tried to sleep. Before he could spiral further, a warm hand slipped up his shoulder, squeezing gently.

"Hey." Ellie's eyes bored into his. "This." She tapped the pages in front of them. "It's a good thing. You've produced an amazing plan. Combined with all the rest..." She shook her head. "I feel like we've got a real chance to make it for the first time in years. It may even draw some of our people back to us. And for that, I'm grateful."

Warmth spread through Grant's chest as he slid his arm around her shoulders and kissed her temple. "I'm just glad I found someone like you."

They sat for a moment, entwined. Then, clearing her throat, Ellie pulled her throat. "None of this will happen if we don't get back to work." She forced a short laugh.

"Right." Grant turned back to the pages, still swimming in front of him, and picked up a pen, fiddling with it. "You've mentioned bringing people back. And Herb..." Ellie glanced up at him. "... seemed a little on edge earlier."

She shrugged, stubbornly silent.

"What are you thinking about?" As she shifted in her seat, he pressed more. "Or should I say, who?" A flare of jealousy licked through his gut.

She waved a hand. "It's nothing."

He rolled his eyes. "We've already established that it's not 'nothing' when you say that."

She glared at him. "Fine. I mean Lorene, Jackie's sister." Sitting back in her chair, she brushed a strand of hair out of her eyes. "It was a big deal when she left— upset a lot of people."

"And what does Herb have to do with it?" Grant swiped a hand across the page, wiping away eraser shavings.

"He and Lorene and Ruffin were real tight. You could call 'em best buds. Lorene and Ruffin were dating." Ellie picked at a hangnail. "He was tangled up in the middle when Lorene ditched Ruffin just before he deployed and high-tailed it out of town. They're cool now, but things have never been the same."

Grant whistled. "I can imagine. Sounds complicated." He studied Ellie. "How do you know all this?"

She chewed her lip. "Me and Lorene and Lou Ellen and Vada were all pretty close. Me and Lou Ellen drove Lorene to the bus station in Cleveland. Vada never quite forgave us, although I've managed to patch things up with her since. She and Lou Ellen don't speak anymore though."

The politics of small towns never ceased to fascinate Grant. He settled back in his seat, wiggling to relieve the numbness that was beginning to prick his backside. "Why didn't you and Jackie ever have a falling out?"

Propping her feet up on the table and pulling a binder onto her lap, Ellie sighed. "Jackie always knew her sister was going to leave. Midnight Bluff didn't have the excitement that Lorene craved—she imagined herself important and successful. Somewhere with a nightlife that she could be seen. She'd never have felt... settled here."

She yanked the rings open with a pop and inserted some more pages. "Honestly, we were all shocked that Lorene made it to nineteen to leave." With a snap, she closed it again. "The

Chapter 20

only person who thought she'd stay was Ruffin. He was over the moon for her. Ready to marry her, have babies. The whole nine."

"As teenagers?" Grant's jaw slackened at the thought. He'd been such an idiot at nineteen. He couldn't imagine being ready to marry and settle down.

"We like to start young in the boonies." Ellie grinned at him. "Some of us anyway."

He licked his lips. "Why do you think she'd come back now?"

"Homesickness. Nostalgia. Tired of hopping from town to town." Ellie shrugged. "Life hasn't been too kind to her. Big city living can be hard when you come from dirt."

"I imagine you'd do alright." Grant smiled at her, thinking of how charming her Southern belle ways would be in Wisconsin.

She shivered. "Big cities give me the heebies. Nope. Give me a simple life in the country, thank you, where I know all my neighbors."

He blinked. Not the reaction he'd imagined. Frowning, he looked down at the papers spread in front of him. "You don't think you'd like living in a city? There's so much to do. Lots of great food, theaters, museums, art galleries."

She bit her pen then shook her head. "That's alright for, like, a short visit. But how do you ever relax with that many people around? There's so little space. Everything gets so dirty. All the traffic. You have to go so far just to see some real nature." Spreading her hands, she smiled. "Not like here. Nature's all around us."

"If you like mosquitoes." He thought of the heat and humidity, the pollen count. How did she love this place so fiercely? Sure, Midnight Bluff had its charms, but as a place to live forever, he wasn't so sure.

"It's got its quirks." With a laugh, she hunched over her binder. "But it's home."

Staring at her, Grant's stomach twisted. Home. That was Midnight Bluff for her. But his career was back in Wisconsin, everything he'd worked so hard for. He pushed the takeout container away, not hungry anymore.

* * *

The sun slanted down the sky, slicking the buildings in amber and honey hues. Ellie stretched her arms overhead, willing the kinks in her back to unwind. Beside her, Grant fiddled with his phone, still absorbed by work mode.

He'd been rather quiet on her the rest of the afternoon. Maybe her jab about city living had hit a little below the belt? With Grant, she always felt off-kilter. One minute he was talking about raising a family in a small town; the next he was praising the virtues of the big city. He was frustratingly inconsistent. She rolled her shoulders, thinking.

"Hey! What you got going this weekend?" She tapped his arm. With a bunch of viewings lined up for a couple farmers, and the usual lookie-loos for one of Herb's storefronts, it would be the perfect time for him to get out and meet more members of the community, see the people who made Midnight Bluff tick.

Plus, she was dead curious about his taste in music. She already had her FM radio queued up to a dozen different stations.

"Hmm? Oh. Polishing up this report. Want to have it ready to show Patty by Monday so we'll be ready for the investors

Chapter 20

she has coming." His voice droned out in a monotone as he typed away at his phone.

Disappointment bloomed in her chest, like tea steeping through hot water. She tucked a piece of hair behind her ear. "Well, if you find yourself needing some fresh air…"

He shoved the phone into his briefcase, glancing down the sidewalk toward their parked cars. "Oh definitely. Going to throw on my sneakers and hit the trails. Go for a run." He finally turned and winked at her. "Work out some of this pent-up energy. No better feeling than feet pounding the pavement."

Heat flashed through Ellie down to her toes. Her eyes scanned down his frame. So that's how he kept that lean body, with a little poun… Nope. She snapped her eyes back up to his to find a wide grin on his face, his teeth shining in the sun.

"Well, I'll let you get to it then. Call me if you need a break from work!" She scooted down the sidewalk like a pack of the town gossips were after her.

Grant's chuckle floated after her. "Oh, I will." As she jolted down Main Street, she glanced in the rear-view mirror to find him waving at her—still with that dazzling grin plastered across her face. In the quiet of her car, a smile of her own tiptoed across her lips.

Chapter 21

Grant tossed his briefcase onto the couch and slumped down next to it. His back ached from a long day hunched over the conference table. He eyed his sneakers, kicked under a chair across the room. With so much on his plate, he hadn't gone running in days and his body was screaming at him to get some of the tension out and clear his head.

A smile tugged at his lips. If he got enough done after his run tonight, tomorrow he could knock off for a few hours to see what Ellie was up to. Her offer of fresh air sounded like a much-needed outing.

Just as he was digging his shoes out from their banishment, his cellphone tolled at him. Groaning, he slapped at the phone on the coffee table, managing to whack the speaker on.

"Graa-aant!" Todd's voice sing-songed over the staticky line. Grimacing, Grant crouched next to the table, running his hands through his hair. Todd was the last person he wanted to talk to right now.

Chapter 21

"What's up, Todd?" He ran his hands through his hair, realizing he'd forgotten to put pomade in this morning. It was kinda nice not to have his hands come away all tacky.

"What's eating you? You nailed this proposal for us man. You should be pumped, man!"

Squeezing his eyes closed, Grant took a breath. He couldn't afford for Todd to think he was off now. Knowing his luck, they'd fly someone in to make the investor pitch at the last second and snatch the credit right out from under him. "It's nothing—I'm stoked. You know how I am—been burning the midnight oil making sure this investor meeting is a cinch."

"Great! Great." Todd cleared his throat, the sound phlegmy and thick. "Look, that's why I've called. We think you've done a solid job. Real solid, compared to what it was. But…"

Grant looked longingly at the window where the last rays of late afternoon sunshine were beginning to slip away. A "but" was never good. It always meant the partners were going to ask for something extraordinarily stupid and unnecessary—and that "special touch" usually meant hours of extra work.

The line crackled, silent. He'd left Todd hanging unprompted too long. That man liked his dramatic pauses. Grant coughed. "You there, Todd?"

"Oh, umm, yeah…" He grinned at the fluster in the other man's voice. "Look, I'm sorry to be the bearer of bad news. But the partners want a ten-year projection added to the plan. Something to jazz up these numbers for the investors—get 'em hyped." He rushed to add as Grant tried to cut in, "And I agree! I think it will impress the investors that are coming and show the council how serious we are about their future."

He dropped his voice. "Grant, pull this off and there's talk of giving you the El Paso project."

Taken For Granted

Grant froze. The El Paso project was their biggest job to date. Whoever headed it up would be managing hundreds of millions in multiple grant projects and not only have an assistant (something he'd been aiming at for years) but an entire team with them on the ground. It was the ultimate carrot to dangle. The breath whooshed out of him.

His thoughts skipped to Ellie and her eyes smiling up at him from the sidewalk. Getting this done would mean not seeing her this weekend. He had to stay focused. Scrubbing his hands through his hair, he tugged at the roots.

"That got your attention, huh?" Todd chuckled. "That meeting is Thursday, right? Lock it in for us and we'll have you on the first plane home out of Memphis on Friday."

"Friday?" Shock tremored through. This was too soon. There was no way he could wrap everything up in time to make sure the next guy handled Midnight Bluff… like he would. The possessiveness of the thought surprised him. An image of Ellie's face clouded his vision. How could he leave her behind? In less than a week, he'd never see her again—off to Wisconsin then Texas then God only knew where.

Todd mistook his surprise for elation. "Too good for words, eh? I'll let the partners know you're on board." Grant sputtered, unable to articulate that he needed more time, so much more time for everyone he'd come to care about. But against Todd's fakely glib voice, the words wouldn't come out. Todd closed the conversation, oblivious. "Look, I got to go. I know you'll be doubling down on this. Keep me posted."

Grant managed to unstick his jaw in time to say, "Will do," before the line clicked. He stared at the phone, rubbing a hand back and forth across his mouth. The El Paso project. His head buzzed, overfilled with conflicting emotions. Why would they

Chapter 21

give him the El Paso project for landing a small-town contract? He shook his head. It made no sense.

But if that's what the big bosses wanted to do, who was he to question such a gift? He drummed his fingers on the coffee table, nerves jangling at him. The gift just better dang well be worth it, to pass up what little time he had left with Ellie.

Ellie. He'd have to tell Ellie. How was he supposed to tell the woman he loved that he had to leave, knowing she wouldn't come with him?

Groaning with frustration, he stood, back cracking. He grabbed his shoes and headed for the door. Figuring out the mess that life had just thrown at him could wait until after his run. Right now, if he didn't move, he was going to spontaneously combust with all the pent-up aggravation. Casting one more glance at his phone, he headed for the door.

* * *

Ellie checked the volume on her phone for the fifth time, fiddling with the buttons to make sure she hadn't accidentally muted it. If Grant called, she didn't want it muffled in her pocket or backpack where she couldn't hear.

Mrs. Betty Coleman chuckled behind her. "I know that look." She stood in the middle of a sunken living room, a truly hideous green shag carpet spread underneath her feet. "You've got a man on the mind." She set a hand weathered from long hours in the field on her hip and nodded. "'Bout time too."

"It's not like that!" Ellie shook her head.

"You don't have to explain to me, sugar. The blush on your face says enough." Mrs. Coleman waved her off as she wandered around the living room, examining the bare walls. "Good foundation?"

Ellie thought of her banter with Grant, their easy camaraderie as they worked together. "Huh, oh yeah. Extra steel in the slab, double-thick concrete. Yazoo clay can't touch this baby. Custom job at the first owner's request. Reinforced with lime."

Nodding, Mrs. Coleman continued her circuit. "Well, I can't say much for their taste in decorating, but the house itself seems solid enough. Everything else is cosmetic. Nothing a little elbow grease can't fix." She patted her sinewy bicep.

Ellie leaned in the doorframe, mind skipping to Grant's pomaded hair and stiff shirts. Her lips twitched into a smile at the thought. "I'm surprised you didn't want to rebuild after the tornado. Insurance money and all."

Mrs. Coleman shot her a look. "Honey, I got more important things to do than argue over the correct width of porches and whether or not a kitchen must have an island." She waved a hand. "Here, the worst we can get into is tile or laminate for the floor and what color of paint." Touching the side of her nose, she added, "I've learned from hard experience that if you don't want to fight, don't create situations for headbutting in the first place. And that takes knowing yourself real well."

Ellie laughed. She'd worked with Mrs. Coleman before as she'd slowly expanded her farm. The lady had strong opinions—reigning them in must be a full-time job in and of itself. Following her as Mrs. Coleman strode into the kitchen, boots echoing on the floor, she leaned against a counter while Mrs. Coleman poked into the cabinets. She gazed down at her silent phone and chewed at her lip.

A hand gently encircled her wrist. "Sugar, if he's keeping

Chapter 21

you waiting, he might not be worth it. The right man will be *running* after you." Mrs. Coleman smiled. "There shouldn't be any game playing."

Shaking her head, Ellie slid the phone into her backpack. "It's not like that. He told me he'd be busy this weekend." She scratched her nose, trying to keep some professionalism in place. "I was just hoping he'd change his mind."

Narrowing her eyes, Mrs. Coleman tilted her head. "Is this that fancy city slicker Patty brought in?"

Ellie pinched her lips together, as flutters tremored through her stomach. She had no idea how the people of Midnight Bluff would react if she and Grant became a thing—not that there was a future for them. The flutters in her stomach stilled and plummeted.

Across from her, Mrs. Coleman grinned. "I knew it. Y'all were looking awful cozy at Al's the other night after the big meeting." She tapped a finger on her lips. "He's got that nice clean-shaven thing going for him too. I can see why you'd be into that."

Trying to smile, Ellie choked out a laugh. "We're not... It's not like that."

Her grin broadened. "Uh-huh." She winked. "Say nothing more. I won't tease you about it." She tapped her arm with one finger. "Except that it would be nice to see you finally have some happiness of your own, dear. You deserve it." Ellie swallowed, trying not to let her eyes cloud at the thought of Grant leaving soon. He'd never hidden that from her.

Mrs. Coleman shoved away from the counter and stood up. "Now. Let's go see that primary bedroom." She hollered over her shoulder as she disappeared down the hall. "Gotta make sure it has what I asked for."

Ellie swiped at her eyes and cleared her throat. "Oh, it does because…"

"Two sinks and separate closets are the keys to a happy marriage!" Mrs. Coleman sing-songed in unison with her down the hall. Ellie snorted and followed, wishing that her happy marriage didn't look like it was becoming more and more of an impossibility.

* * *

Children's laughter from the yard echoed up to Grant as he slumped over his computer typing away at projections. He glanced at the window and the sunlight sliding in. Was Ellie showing a property to some hot farmer right now, exchanging witty banty about tractors and plowing? He gritted his teeth and reached for his briefcase—he needed the notes she'd written up on the railroad tract.

As he snatched them out of an inner pocket, another flotilla of papers slid out and dashed to the floor. With a grumble, he slid out of his chair, knees crackling, and knelt. As he shuffled the papers back together, a photograph wedged among them caught his eye. He plucked the Polaroid-sized photo out and examined it.

The Yellow-Rumped Warbler that Ellie had photographed at Hey Joe's in Cleveland twinkled up at him, its feathers gleaming in the crisp afternoon sun of the photo. The picture must have gotten mixed in with his papers somehow. He brushed a finger across the shiny surface, marveling at the delicate spray of feathers, the way the light highlighted the bird's merry bobbing on the beam. How she'd captured such

Chapter 21

life and breath in one snap took his breath away.

She was so extraordinarily talented. And in a few days, he'd be leaving her behind in a town he'd come to love like it was his home.

His breath hitched.

This was not at all how he imagined his life going. Finding the perfect woman and settling down was supposed to come after he'd landed the big promotion, gotten his life straightened out. Not like this. Not when achieving his dreams meant...

His hand shook as he looked at the photo. Straightening his shoulders, he swallowed. What was done, was done. No use crying over it. He tossed it onto the pile of detritus headed for the garbage can after this.

A second later, he snatched it back and carefully tucked it into his billfold. Maybe, he could convince Ellie to come with him to Madison. It was a long shot; she loved Midnight Bluff as a part of herself. But he had to try.

He turned back to his computer, breathing deeply through his nose, trying to settle himself. Time to finish this and get the heck out of here. And if Ellie wouldn't come with him—why linger where he'd only ever experienced love to have it snatched away?

Chapter 22

Ellie's fingers hovered over the keypad, itching to tap out "You here?" The weekend's text string glowed on the screen, Grant's one-word responses to her funny quips and memes about country life halting her message. She was *not* going to be one of those girls who turned to mush over a guy. Dumping the phone into her backpack, she stomped out of the truck and into the courthouse.

As she rounded the corner into the conference room, she skidded to a halt inside the door, perturbed. Grant sat at the table already, coffee cups and pastries spread before him, clearly arranged for her to sit beside him. And he was in a full suit. Clean-shaven with pomade slicking back his hair. Gone was the sexy shadow of stubble on his jaw. A subtle whiff of his orange and sandalwood cologne drifted to her, stirring something deep in her chest.

Snorting, she took a chair across and down from him. "Worried about a windstorm?"

He patted at his hair as he frowned, his eyes measuring the

Chapter 22

distance between them. Slowly, he handed her a cup of coffee. "Not particularly." He slid a danish to her.

"Then what's with the suit?" She waved a hand at the impeccably tailored ensemble, telling herself that he looked ridiculous in it. Hastily, she stuffed a bite of danish in her mouth. Ridiculously handsome, that is.

Blinking, he looked down at himself, the jacket cutting perfectly across his svelte shoulders. A twinge of guilt twisted her mouth, but she took a sip of her scalding coffee to cover it. In for a penny, in for a pound now.

He looked back up, the crinkle between his eyebrows deepening. "Just trying to look professional is all." Staring back at her for a second longer, she wondered if he was about to demand an apology. Instead, he shook his head and pulled a binder from his briefcase.

"Let's get to work, shall we?"

That was it? No chit-chat. No "how was your weekend." Just nose to the grindstone, like they were merely work chums. She took a deep breath in, nostrils flaring. "Sure. Let's get to work."

He began flipping through the binder, a much more polished version of the drafts and notes they'd come up with the past week. Graphics and charts adorned the pages, highlighting just how much thought had gone into this plan. This was so much more polished than the rough-and-ready version they had presented to the council. For a few minutes, Ellie sat lost in wonder, as Grant flipped the pages, leaning across the table to show her different items and ask her thoughts on certain points.

This was good. Really good. From creating a cleaned-up, more vibrant downtown, to crafting an engaging online presence and community-led Chamber of Commerce campaign. She skimmed over their proposed schedule of festivals and studied the rural tourism outlay featuring Dottie's "cabins." This plan incorporated all their ideas, including the nature trail and proposed co-working space. A list of other defunct properties that were available for renovation was also included as high-value investment opportunities, her contact info included neatly at the bottom of the page. Ellie sucked in a breath.

"All of this…" She blinked, trying to keep her vision clear. "It's so much." Coughing, she looked up at Grant. "No wonder you were busy this weekend."

The frown deepened as he avoided her eyes. "That's not all of it." Flipping the page, he pointed at a colorful graph. Bars traced Midnight Bluff's trajectory a decade into the future. A future filled with growth, prosperity, and stability. With people brimming in the streets of the town once more.

And Grant had created this path all by himself. Her eyes traced over it. "What? Are you…" She looked up, hope fluttering in her stomach. "Are you saying you'll be here for ten years, seeing this through?"

He sat back and shook his head. "No." She watched his throat work, as he glanced out the door and down the hall. "I'll… I'll be leaving at the end of the week."

Weight toppled onto Ellie, pressing her into the chair. "But… I thought you'd be here for weeks yet." She squirmed trying to breathe. "You said there would be a lot to put into place once the proposal was accepted."

Grimacing, he nodded. "Yeah. Well, my bosses want me back in Wisconsin. They'll send someone else out to see to the…" He waved a hand. "Follow up."

Chapter 22

Heat, blinding and white, in its intensity, surged through her. "So that's it? You're here as, what? A closer? Seal the deal and get the heck out of dodge?" Her hands shook and she stood, putting distance between them. Her coffee cup flew over. With a yelp, Grant snatched the binder away from the darkly spreading puddle.

"Was everything you said just a lie to get me to help you?"

He paused in his frantic patting of napkins. "What? No! Of course not." He circled the table to grab her hands, his sticky with coffee and cream. "I never intended to… Ellie, I meant, mean, everything I said. Just… things came together a lot more quickly than I expected."

"Than you expected. What does that mean?" She was shaking now. With rage and a deep, rending pain she didn't want to, couldn't name.

Shoving his hands into his hair, Grant stared at the ceiling. "I was at the end of my rope when you started helping me. I was about to lose not only this contract but my job. Then you walk in and…"

He waved at her. "…and look at you. You're incredible. You're so passionate and you're whip-smart. It's like a switch flipped. You made things fit. Everything just fell into place."

A forest fire seared through her chest, blinding her with its flames. All these words, and he'd already made up his mind.

He dropped his hands, leaving his hair in spikes. "My bosses. They've offered me a job. It's life changing. If I don't take it… It's everything I've been working for. And you made it happen." With a crack, she felt her heart split itself in two.

She looked up at him through tears. What she was hearing couldn't be true. He couldn't be leaving because of her. Not him. He couldn't be leaving her behind too. Pressing her hands to her cheeks, she whispered. "Stop saying that."

He reached out and squeezed her hands. "Hey. Just because it's different doesn't mean it's bad. We can figure things out. You could come with me." He said it so casually, like leaving behind her home was nothing. With that, things crystallized for her, the hole in her chest a reminder that she couldn't depend on anyone but herself.

"We." She let the word drop flatly. Snatching her hands away. "There is no we."

Yanking her backpack up, the strap finally gave way, yanking loose from the bottom with a soft rip that left her stumbling. Grant reached out to steady her. With a sob, she hugged the abused bag to her chest to ward off his hands and dashed for the door.

His voice echoed after her down the hall, calling her name, but he didn't come after her. Mrs. Coleman's words echoed in her head: *The right man will be running after you.* The thought punched into her, sinking an ache so deep into her chest she didn't think it would ever go away. But she couldn't waver now. Clutching her backpack closer, she stepped outside.

The sunlight slapped into her as she tilted her chin up and marched down the steps, not caring about the tears tracking down her cheeks. What a fool she'd been for thinking they might be able to find a future together.

Well, she'd learned her lesson. And she wouldn't make that mistake again. Slamming the door of her truck shut behind her, she revved the engine and headed home alone.

* * *

Chapter 22

Grant dropped back into the chair, his legs rubbery, as the front door of the courthouse slammed shut on his seared nerves. She hadn't even paused as she stormed out, to give him a chance to explain more, to apologize. To beg her to go with him.

He tugged at his hair, sure that any minute steam would roll off his skin. He had worked so hard for this promotion—for it to go so utterly, miserably wrong. His stomach knotted painfully at the thought of the look on her face.

He had told her the truth. What more could he do? The glare of the table was beginning to burn into his eyes. In a burst of energy, he shoved away from the table and began to pace.

Before he had finished his first circuit, Mr. Pearce poked his head in the room. Shocked, Grant froze, nearly tripping over his own pant leg.

"May I help you?"

With a sharp wave, Mr. Pearce brushed aside his question. "You screwed up."

"Wh... What?"

"You heard me. You screwed up." He jabbed a finger at the papers on the table. "I don't know what you've got going that you think is more important than a chance at real happiness..." He pointed a shaking hand towards the direction of the front door where Ellie had just disappeared. Grant belatedly remembered that Mr. Pearce had been her foster father. He softened at the realization of how much their argument must have torn up the older man. "...but let me tell you, nothing—nothing—is more than the woman you love. Not money. Not career. Not even friends and family. You messed up, son."

Breath gusted out of Grant as he leaned against the table. "I know."

Mr. Pearce waved his arms in front, exasperated. "Then man up and do something about it. Go after her!"

Slumping back into his chair, Grant shrugged. "Why bother? I can't fix anything—I can't make this... situation... magically disappear."

Mr. Pearce stared at him from beneath rather wooly eyebrows. "If that's how you see it, then you've already lost her."

Throwing his hands in the air, Grant said, "That's kind of the point! I don't have a choice here—I'm out of options."

Shaking his head, Mr. Pearce shoved his hands in his pocket. "We always have a choice. We just have to have the guts to make it."

Before Grant could ask him what he meant, the older man spun on his heel and walked off, his footsteps echoing down the hall. Grant stared after him. In the year he'd been here, that was the most he'd ever heard him speak. He *hmmed* in surprise. Miracles happen.

If only a miracle could save him from this mess.

Chapter 23

Grant stared at all the materials spread out on the table. Taking a sip of his coffee, he winced at its coldness, the milk having gone off. He'd have to walk over to the bakery and get another. He sighed and swiped his hands over his face, not sure where to begin without Ellie. She had guided him through so much—he hadn't realized the extent he'd been relying on her.

A soft knocking on the door behind him made him spin around. Mayor Patty stood in the doorway, a shining broach pinned on one shoulder and a smile on her face.

"Oh dear, you look like you've been burning the candle at both ends." She pulled out a chair and sat next to him.

"If that's anything like burning the midnight oil, then yes, yes I've been at it." He tried to smile at her, but his mouth wobbled then flattened. Even his body was betraying him today.

She patted his arm. "I won't keep you long, but I wanted to sneak a peek at the presentation, if you don't mind. I'd love to see it before you show it to our investors."

"Of course. Your name will be on it. Best foot forward and all that." He flipped to the first page of the binder and slid it to her. She grinned at him and began flipping pages, *hmming* and *ahhing* to herself.

Her face lit up. "I didn't know you'd spoken with Mr. Stevens!" She tapped a page. "This is wonderful. Just wonderful!" She touched his arm. "Renovating the old plant—it breathes life back into this town. And how you've tied in the railroad." She covered her mouth with her hand, brown eyes shining.

He squirmed in his chair. So much of this wouldn't have happened without Ellie. She should be here with him to see this unfolding. He stared at her abandoned pastry, willing her to walk back in.

"Grant! This is marvelous. It's… It's better than I imagined. People living along Main Street. The brick streets restored not just replaced." She swallowed, her throat working. "Excuse me. It's just been so long since I've had hope, real hope, that this place could be a spark of what it was." She looked up at him. "And this is more. Thank you." Her eyes traced the direction of his gaze, the forlorn danish, and softened.

Lowering her voice, she said, "She'll come around. Have faith." The whole building must have heard their argument.

Shaking his head, he coughed, forcing a chuckle. Now was not the time to bemoan his love life. He had a job to do. "I'm glad you like the presentation." He waved a hand. "There's more."

As she flipped the pages, he explained, "My bosses wanted me to add some projections to help you impress your investors—demonstrate the viability of this project over the long-term."

Chapter 23

Mayor Patty's mouth twisted in a rueful smile as she landed on the colorful chart. Rocking back and forth, she let out a cackle. "Someone did their research. This is just the sort of thing that gets ole' Dale's motor going." She shook her head, still smiling.

"Dale?"

"Dale Ernst. A friend from my college days at Ole Miss."

Dale Ernst. The billionaire. The name hit Grant like a ton of bricks. Suddenly the offer of the El Paso project made sense. They didn't care about Grant or his work or if he landed the contract for this backwater town at the end of the day. What they really wanted was to impress Dale Ernst.

Bringing on a partner like Dale Ernst would allow the company to grow in unimagined ways. And money like that always came with strings attached. Grant pressed a hand over his mouth. This was what they'd had him spend his last few days in Midnight Bluff on? Going in blind to impress a potential partner.

They wouldn't... It clicked. They were going to send someone. Probably Todd or even someone else higher up. Clenching his fist, he looked back at the chart. Let Grant do all the work; let someone else take all the glory.

And, as always, Grant lost everything in the bargain.

Mayor Patty's hand on his arm drew him back from his spiral. "You look pretty far away there."

He worked his tongue across the top of his dry mouth. "A few things are just making more sense to me now. I was not... informed about Mr. Ernst."

Her lips pressed together. "I see." She glanced down at the chart then flipped the binder shut. "Well, I'm no stranger to politickin.' For what it's worth, you've proven to me that you have more integrity than a house full of preachers."

Pain lanced through Grant's chest. "I don't… Thank you, but I don't deserve that." He'd let himself stray so far from who he had always meant to be. First, with all the stunts he'd pulled with Cress. Then wallowing in his misery. Now, he'd let Ellie down. How was that acting with integrity?

She patted his leg. "Not many men would stick to their word when it was this hard to achieve. You've been away from home for the better part of a year. Had your heart handed back to ya' by one woman and lost it to another." Shaking her head, she continued, "And you still haven't given up."

"Of course not. I gave my word."

Pointing at him, she grinned. "See? That's integrity."

He shook his head, not seeing her point, and she shrugged. "Argue with me all you want, but I'm right. And that's why I have something else to talk to you about."

Sitting up a little straighter, he nodded. "Alright." He could use something else to do to take his mind off things.

"I want to offer you a job."

He blinked at her. He couldn't be hearing right. "A job?"

Smiling, she nodded. "Our town planner position has been empty for over a decade. I'd like you to take the position." She waved a hand. "I'll find the funds somewhere to cover the salary. But if we're going to do this…" Tapping the binder, she winked at him. "…Successfully, I'd like someone who knows what they're doing *here* to see that it gets done."

A cool wave washed over Grant, buoying him. Staying in Midnight Bluff, seeing his plan through, being with Ellie—it was more than he could ask for. Yearning struck him as he thought of the little house they'd fill with laughter and warmth, the friends they'd see filling the sidewalks. The children that

Chapter 23

would fill their lives with chaos and joy.

He bowed his head as he struggled against the longing that filled his chest. It would mean giving up his life in Wisconsin. The career he'd worked so hard for. A chance to change the landscape of the country.

But changing this one corner of the world might be enough. Sometimes, the smallest changes had the biggest impact.

Mr. Pearce's words echoed in his head: *We always have a choice. We just have to have the guts to make it.* Well, here was the choice.

"Can I have some time? To consider." He needed to go for a walk. Think about it.

"Of course, hon. It's a big decision. Just let me know by the meeting Wednesday." With one more pat on his knee, she stood and swooped out, hallooing to various people as she made her way down the hall.

Knowing he wasn't going to get any more work done for a while, he scooped all his papers into his briefcase, dumped the cold coffees and uneaten pastries into the trash, and headed for the door. Fresh air was what he needed. And fresh coffee.

Beelining for the Loveless Bakery, he hopped over cracked sidewalks and pitted bricks. It was a wonder the sky hadn't clouded over with how thunderous he was feeling, but the sun continued to beat his back despite the lightning storm brewing in his chest.

With a nerve-rattling jangle, the bells above the door announced his entrance. Willow thumped down a tray of uniced cupcakes and crossed her arms, narrowing her eyes. She ran her tongue over her teeth. So, Ellie had been here. Grant winced.

"I ain't got nothin' to say to you." Willow picked up a piping bag and began swirling pink flourishes onto the cupcakes. Somehow, she was still managing to glare at him, even as she carefully iced each dessert.

Grant rubbed at his eyes with his fingertips. Willow was one of the few people in this town who'd always tolerated him; he couldn't take being on her bad side. "I already know I messed up with Ellie—Mr. Pearce gave me an earful about it."

Her mouth twitched as she frowned over the cupcakes. "I imagine he did. You deserve that, and a butt-kicking too. I have half a mind to do it myself." He clenched his fists at his sides, every inch of his body knotted with tension.

"C'mon, Will. Please don't be like that. I've got enough on my mind without worrying over you being mad at me too." He looked out the window, back at the courthouse. "Lots to decide."

Willow *hmmed* in her throat as she followed his gaze. Pointing the piping bag at him, she said, "Well, if you want to get back on my good side, you better start with a big ole' apology to Ellie. I don't know what you said to her this morning, but I know that girl. She does *not* cry over men, and she was bawling over you."

Grant's stomach twisted up into a painful knot. He'd never meant to get attached... His gaze drifted back to the courthouse. "Could I get a cup of coffee, to-go?"

With a sniff, Willow stared at him.

"Please, Willow? You have good reason to be mad, but as I said, I've got a lot to think over, and I'm too tired to do it with a level head right now." She tilted her chin and raised her eyebrows meaningfully. He sighed. "I promise I'll apologize to Ellie as soon as she'll take my calls again."

Willow nodded curtly and turned to fill a to-go cup for him.

Chapter 23

Grant sagged with relief. With Mayor Patty's words buzzing in his mind, he needed to find a quiet place to think. And if his experience with the gossip mill was any indicator, that wouldn't be in Midnight Bluff.

* * *

Grant chunked his briefcase onto the table and slumped onto the sofa. Kicking his shoes off, he drug his feet up onto the couch, not caring if his clothes got wrinkled. He grabbed a throw pillow and hugged it to his chest.

He'd known Ellie was going to be upset, but he'd thought they could at least talk about things… With realizing that one of the suits would be swooping in to try to scoop his account and now Mayor Patty offering him a job, his brain felt like a computer stuck in overdrive. And the only person who could help him parse it all out, he couldn't even talk to.

He pushed the pillow over his face and groaned. With a huff, he sat up then shuffled around the room. What he needed was a snack. Something to nosh on while he debated.

He swiped a legal pad out of his briefcase on his way to the tiny kitchen. Maybe a pros and cons list would help too. Opening the refrigerator, he recoiled from the greyed and congealed… whatever… was growing in the plethora of takeout containers. With a grunt, he slammed the door and opened the freezer. A single frozen burrito greeted him in its shiny plastic wrapper. It would have to do.

As the microwave hummed, he drew a line down the page then divided it in half to make the top section his pros and the bottom section his cons. Scribbling Midnight Bluff and

Madison, Wisconsin, at the top of the page on either side, he stared at the blank yellow expanse, tapping the pen to his lips. These things never worked unless he was honest with himself.

On the pros side for Midnight Bluff, he wrote, "Ellie." He paused. If she would even talk to him after this. His hand shook as he quickly filled out the rest of the page while he chewed on the half-frozen burrito.

Sitting back down on the couch, he stared at the list. He doodled stars and squiggly lines around different points that meant more to him, as his mind wondered. What would it be like to live in Midnight Bluff? He could picture strolling up to the courthouse every day, cup of coffee in hand, cajoling the barest crack of a smile out of Mr. Pearce, taking lunch breaks with Ellie out in the square, that blasted sun beating down. Behind him, the door crashed open.

He spun around to find a tiny blond boy and even tinier girl sprawled across his doorstep. The boy howled while the little girl beat his shins. "I told you he was in here! Now, look what ya' done." Grant stood as the children scrambled up.

"I just wanted to see what was up here!" The little boy shoved her off and stood up, hands on hips and eyes darting around. He shrugged at Grant's open-mouthed stare. "Dad never lets us up here."

Footsteps boomed up the stairs behind them. "Kids! If you're up here no dessert for a…"

Mr. Tisdale stopped at the sight of Grant, hand comically frozen in midair with the index finger pointed upward.

"Mr. Emberson!" He snatched the kids by the ears back out the apartment, grimaces scrawled across their faces. Grant winced in sympathy. "We didn't know you were home!"

"Apparently, neither did these peeping Toms." He forced a

Chapter 23

chuckle. "It's alright, Ed. I wanted to walk a little, so I parked around the corner."

The little boy piped up. "We just wanted a peek, Daddy. We weren't trying to get in. The door fell."

Mr. Tisdale looked to Grant for an explanation. With a shrug, Grant offered, "I must not have latched the door all the way behind me." He shook his head. "Kids will be kids."

With a huff, Mr. Tisdale released the kids with a point back down the stairs. They scrambled away. "Sorry about that. They've been extra rowdy lately."

"No harm done." He tossed the legal pad onto the table and crossed his arms; he was in for a long conversation now. "Kids learn by messing up."

"Same can be said for adults." Mr. Tisdale nodded. His eyes zeroed in on the legal pad and he stepped forward, oblivious to his intrusion. "What's this?"

Groaning to himself, Grant cursed not putting his list someplace out of sight. "Just… trying to make a decision."

With a twinkle in his eye, Mr. Tisdale skimmed a finger down the page. "Looks like your mind is already made up."

Grant looked at him, startled. "What do you mean?"

He tapped the page. "Look at what you've circled the most."

Grant picked up the legal pad, letting his eyes truly see it for the first time. While he'd starred his parents back in Wisconsin and his job, he'd circled and squiggled so many things in Midnight Bluff. And around Ellie's name… He sucked in a breath.

A dark ring of blue ballpoint pen completely encircled her, the line traced over and over. All the other stars paled next to her.

Mr. Tisdale patted his shoulder. "So, what are you going to

do?"

Grant grinned at him. "I'm going to go get her."

* * *

"Oh, honey, why are you even calling me about this?" Grant's eyes filled at his mother's voice. "Your dad and I will be fine. More than fine. I'm just so happy for you."

"Well, it's not a done deal yet. I've got to see how she feels about it." He scuffed at the carpet with his barefoot while Ed tromped through the front door with a pan full of tacos and the biggest grin he'd ever seen. He guessed they were… friends… now? At least the other man seemed to be exuberantly making himself at home while Leila and Danny screeched joyfully in and out of the loft.

Grant had to admit, it was a lot more cheerful with all the lights on and people bustling about.

"If even half the things you've told me about her are true, I'm sure things will work themselves out." He could hear her slamming the oven. "Just be patient. I'm sure she has whiplash from this whole situation."

"Yeah." He sighed. "Definitely. She's still not taking my calls."

"Time, baby. It's only been a few hours. Give her some space. Remember, your dad had to woo me for months before I'd go out with him."

Patience was not Grant's forte. "I'll try."

"All right. Keep us in the loop. Love you."

As he hung up, he looked over at Ed, laying out a veritable Mexican fiesta on his tiny table, and tried to quiet the misgivings he felt. He'd prayed for a miracle and gotten it, hadn't he?

Chapter 23

He just had to trust it now.

Chapter 24

Sweat trickled down Ellie's back, making her shirt cling to her stomach and chest. "I'm so sorry, Lou." She set a glass of tea down in front of her friend at the kitchen table then turned to open the hall closet. "The A/C gave out this morning and I just…" She waved at the box fans as she drug them out. There was simply no way to afford repairs right now. Not with what she still owed for having her roof repaired earlier that week.

Sighing, she plunked one of the fans in front of an already open window and plugged it in, *hmming* in relief as tepid air began to stir through the house. Outside, purple martins dipped and dived around their high houses, swinging merrily from the poles she'd erected in the backyard.

Lou Ellen waved a hand. "It's not the first time I've been through a Mississippi heat wave in April, sweetie. It certainly won't be the last." She took a sip of her tea as Ellie drug the other fan across the kitchen next to the table. "But why don't you get that gentleman friend over here to help you? He sure

Chapter 24

looked handy with the heavy equipment a couple of weeks ago."

"Grant?" Ellie scoffed. "Fat lot of help he'd be with a compressor. Not that he'd come anyway." She thought guiltily of the calls she'd let go unheard to voicemail, the phone finally having fallen silent yesterday. It really was over now.

She jammed the plug into the socket, wincing as the dying plug sparked her hand. She turned around just in time to see Lou Ellen burying her nose back into her glass, eyebrows up to her hairline. "What? I see that face." Fisting her hands onto her hips, she shook her head. "We grew up together. I know all your looks."

"It's just…" Lou Ellen winced. "Ok, don't take this the wrong way." Ellie tensed. "But you've been crabby the last couple of days. Are you ever going to tell me what happened? Dad won't say a word—says it's your business."

Squeezing the back of her neck, Ellie considered. Lou Ellen didn't like Grant already. Telling her anything would just give her more fuel for the fire. She looked at her friend's wide eyes, filled with concern and softened. "I just feel so stupid."

"Oh, honey." Lou Ellen patted the chair next to her and Ellie sank into it gratefully as a warm breeze sifted over her skin. A glass of sweet tea slid in front of her, sweating in the heat.

Quietly, she confided in Lou Ellen just like she used to when they were teenagers. "I blurred the lines—I knew he was leaving. He always made that clear. But I just couldn't keep work and personal separate, not with him. And now…"

"He should be ashamed of himself." The words fell bitter and heavy from Lou Ellen's lips.

"Why?" Ellie looked up startled. "I'm the one who read more into it."

Shaking her head, Lou Ellen retorted, "But he was involved as well. He is responsible too. I saw you two together. It wasn't just in your head. Half the town thinks you two are a couple."

Ellie's eyes watered. "We never even talked about it. Whatever it was. It's just over." Rubbing at her face, she hiccupped. "And now, I don't feel like I even get to be upset about it because it wasn't even a thing."

Lou Ellen grabbed her arm. "Nonsense. You get to be upset. Just because you weren't Facebook official doesn't mean it wasn't real and meaningful. No one else gets to tell you how to feel your feelings."

Sniffling, Ellie nodded. "You're right." She sat back, taking a deep breath, and swiping at her face. "I just need to put all this behind me now."

With a nod, Lou Ellen sat back and began rifling through her purse. Intrigued, Ellie looked over. "What are you doing?"

"Just following breakup protocol." She withdrew a long brown bottle from her bag. "Bourbon! Because no heartbreak goes unhammered around here."

Rolling her eyes, Ellie shook her head. "I can't day drink right now, Lou Ellen. I have clients to see this afternoon."

Snickering, Lou Ellen stood and pulled ice cream from the freezer. "It doesn't count if it's frozen, right?"

Ellie's eyes widened. "When did you get that in there?"

"That's a trade secret!"

Hugging her best friend, Ellie sniffed, "I don't know how you manage it, but you're the best person I know."

Lou Ellen threw her head back laughing. "Save that for when Mr. Fixit gets here."

"Lou Ellen! You can't afford to fix my A/C either on a secretary's salary!" She slapped at Lou Ellen's arm, alarmed.

Chapter 24

"Maybe not. But Daddy can!" Holding up her phone, Lou Ellen showed her the glowing string of text messages. "He's already called Mr. Fixit and they're sending someone out." She held up a finger. "Before you argue with me, I didn't ask him to. He did it on his own. You know what he's like."

Sucking on her lower lip, Ellie frowned. "Still. It's too much."

Lou Ellen hugged her again. "You deserve to be taken care of. And who else to do it besides family? Foster or not. Now, let's eat this before it turns into a puddle!"

Just as they sat down to dig into their boozy ice cream, Ellie's phone rang. She nearly slapped it off out of habit from dodging Grant's calls but paused to look at the screen.

"Hey, Patty!" Her voice cracked from her earlier crying jag.

"Ellie, I'm just calling to confirm you'll be at the investor presentation tomorrow morning. It's not like you to ghost on me."

"You know I've been doing all of this pro bono, Patty. Work has picked up, so I don't know if I'll be able to make it." She winced at the white lie. She did have some meetings tomorrow, but not until the afternoon.

"Mmhmm." Mayor Patty let the sound hang long and skeptical in the air. "Anyway, I'm the one who wants you there. You have such a gift. You can convince ice to be warm." No mention of Grant, which was smart on the mayor's part. This lady knew how to politic.

Pinching the bridge of her nose, Ellie sucked in a deep breath. "I'll see what I can do Patty, but no promises."

"I know you won't let me down!" The line clicked.

Ellie sat back in her chair, hands over her face. "Ugh! That woman knows how to lay down a guilt trip thicker than tar."

Swirling her spoon through her ice cream, Lou Ellen, "So,

are you going to go?"

Scooping up a big spoonful, Ellie studied it. "I don't know. I've put so much work into this, and I want to see it through." She shoved the icy sweetness into her mouth. "But I just don't know if I can bear to see Grant." Pain bloomed in her head, and she wasn't sure if it was an ice-cream headache or the certainty of knowing that she had to see him one last time.

* * *

The reassuring smell of butter, sugar, and vanilla wafted over Ellie, calming her jangling nerves. She tugged at the skirt of the slub silk dress Lou Ellen had lent her. "You don't think this is too formal, do you?"

Willow rubbed her shoulders. "Too formal! Nonsense. You look like a million bucks."

Vada patted her shoulder. "Grant can just eat his heart out."

A pit opened in Ellie's stomach. "Oh no! It's too much. He can't be distracted during the presenta…" Willow grabbed her arm as she started rummaging for keys.

"Sugar! Calm yourself." She rubbed her shoulders again. "We're just trying to pep you up. You look good but not too good. Just the right amount of good. Ok?"

Ellie massaged the pressure point between her thumb and index finger, willing her racing heart to slow down. "Ok." She paced back and forth. "I've got my notes. I've got business cards just in case. I've got this." She held up the ancient but still shiny briefcase Mr. Pearce had fished out of the back of a closet after learning about Ellie's backpack malfunction.

Vada waved a hand. "You've got this."

Chapter 24

Ellie paced some more, nodding. "Yep." Grant's face flashed into her mind, and she redoubled her speed.

"If you don't slow down, I'm going to get motion sickness just watching you."

Pausing, Ellie studied Vada. "Why are you here anyway? It can't just be for this amazing pep-talk."

Sipping her coffee, Vada smirked at her. "I take exception to that."

"But shouldn't you be at the Co-Op? Or shoveling horse sh—"

"Hey now! Sometimes I have business to..." Vada air-quoted "*attend to* as well." She exchanged a look with Willow.

Crossing her arms, Ellie waited. Vada pursed her lips. "All right! I'm meeting Pastor Riser. But it is strictly business—something about the youth group. Don't need the town's busybodies getting wind of it and starting any gossip. Or matchmaking." Muttering about people minding their own business, Vada settled into a chair as Ellie resumed her pacing.

Willow flipped the coffee grinder on, the smell of freshly pulverized beans triggering memories of the days she'd spent with Grant, poring over pages, planning for a future they'd never spend together.

Prickles broke out up and down her arms. "Y'all. I can't face him. I just can't." Willow and Vada huddled around her. "How am I supposed to sit in that room, listening to his voice, seeing our work—knowing it's the last time? How am I supposed to say goodbye?"

Willow grabbed her hand. "Take it from me, sugar. If you don't say goodbye to someone you love, no matter how bittersweet, you will always regret it."

Wrapping an arm around Ellie's shoulders, Vada pressed

their temples together. "I've never seen anything that you couldn't do. You've picked yourself up so many times. This will be just a tiny bump in the road. It may feel like a mountain now. But you'll see. You have us to climb it with you."

"I know." Ellie drew a breath in even as her heart quivered at the thought. Then she stood up straight. "Thank you." Trying to work some moisture into her dry mouth, she nodded to herself. "I can do this." Nodding again, she repeated, "I have to do this. For the town."

"Darn straight you can do this." Vada hugged her. "You're one of the strongest women I know." Ellie gasped as Vada shoved her out the door. "And you're late. No more nattering. Go!"

As she hurried across the town square to the courthouse in her ridiculously high heels, she couldn't help but giggle as Vada hollered after her, "You'll do great, honey! Show those men how ladies run the show!"

The shadow of the courthouse fell across her and she looked up at its marble façade, a reminder of good years gone by. And everything Midnight Bluff had to look forward to again. If only she could get through this one meeting. If she could put her wounded heart aside and help Grant land this presentation and the support of these investors. She needed to be cool, calm, and collected—and she couldn't do that if she melted into a puddle of tears at the sight of him

Imagining ice as thick as a cinder block wall around her heart, Ellie rolled her shoulders back and marched up the steps. Her heels clicked against the sparkling tile floor, heralding her arrival. Perfunctorily, she kissed Mr. Pearce on the cheek when he stepped from the old secretary's office to greet her. "I'm ok," she murmured as his eyes searched her face and he

Chapter 24

squeezed her elbow.

Numbing herself, she breezed on down the hall, collecting Mayor Patty in her wake. "Darling, I'm so glad you were able to make it. Today just wouldn't be the same without you! Grant has told me how critical your help has been. He speaks very highly of you."

"Anything for the town, Patty."

They paused at the door to the meeting hall. Mayor Patty touched her shoulder. "I know how... difficult... the last few days have been. Thank you, truly, for coming. Just hang in there for a few more minutes."

Ellie shivered. She bobbed a nod, and Patty ducked through the door.

Pressing a hand over her chest, Ellie sucked in a breath, steadying herself. A step echoed behind her. "I wasn't sure you'd come." Grant's voice rumbled through her, sending microscopic cracks through her frosty guard. She ground her teeth, willing some composure.

"I keep my word." She looked up into his dazzling hazel eyes. The hall tilted, and she reached out and placed a hand on the wall as nonchalantly as possible to prop herself upright. Despite the devastatingly sharp cut of his suit, a faint shadow of stubble shaded his jaw, his hair tousled and free from pomade, tempting her to run her fingers through it.

His eyes traced over her face, flitting back and forth as she forced herself to hold his gaze. The wall around her heart was melting, dripping, and running off her in deepening pools. Under that sizzling gaze, all Grant had to do was touch her and she knew she was a goner. He opened his mouth then shut it again, a wrinkle creasing his brow. "Can we..."

A frigidity rivaling the Arctic washed over her. If that

question included the word "friends," she would take the nearest sharp object and stab it in the middle of his perfectly toned chest. With a haughty sniff, she waved at the door, cutting him off. "Let's just get this over with, shall we?"

She took a step into the room. His hand encircled her wrist, gently tugging her back. In her teetering heels, she was unable to resist and she fell backward out of the door.

With a small gasp, she found herself cradled against Grant's chest, her heart racing against his as the door shielded them from the curious stares of those inside. Heat bloomed in her cheeks at how her sudden entrance and exit must have looked. But right then, she stood paralyzed in Grant's arms as he looked into her eyes.

"We're in this together, right?" He breathed into her ear.

She swallowed, clinging desperately to the last shred of dignity she had. He was leaving. Tomorrow. She couldn't give into this.

Shoving away from his chest, she glared at him. She was a professional. Vada and Willow's words echoed through her. "I can do this."

She turned and strode through the door. Grant slipped in after her. From the podium, Mayor Patty studied them, one eyebrow raised quizzically.

"Now that we're all here, let's begin." Mayor Patty greeted their guests and introduced the row of fastidiously dressed businesspeople already opening their red folders and tucking into the pastries Grant had laid out for them.

Around the room, townspeople and council members murmured as they watched. Suddenly, Ellie was glad that she had "overdressed" for today. She was pretty sure that she spotted a few of the potential investors wearing Burberry, Hermes, and

Chapter 24

one lady appeared to be wearing Prada head to toe.

Her off-the-rack silk dress felt tawdry in comparison. Lifting her chin, she forced a polite smile as the shaking of hands commenced. One older man with diamond cufflinks patted her hand reassuringly and winked. "Dale Ernst." He paused as if he expected her to know him, then smiled widely as she politely offered up her name. "Charming town you have here. Good bones." He waved at the projector Grant was setting up. "Can't wait to see what you have for us today."

Another man with salt and pepper hair pomaded back in a shining slick strolled over to her. "So, you're Grant's local expert I've heard about just now." He cocked his head to the side. Straightening her spine, Ellie offered her hand.

"Ellie Winters. Of Winters Real Estate." Something struck her as off-putting about this guy—a bit vain and condescending.

His mouth twisted to the side in a smirk. "Todd Paxton. Of Renewzit. I'm here to give the presentation today. Gotta put the shine on and all."

"I'd think that would be pretty hard for someone who hasn't been involved at all." The words slipped out of her mouth before she could think. Her knuckles tightened around the handle of her briefcase. What had she just done?

The smile on Todd's face froze. "Well, it's all in the delivery, isn't it? Excuse me." He strode over to Grant and whispered something to him. Grant glanced at her, a suppressed smile on his face. Stress bloomed through her as Grant turned back to the projector then flashed a thumbs-up to Mayor Patty.

Mayor Patty introduced Todd and Ellie dimmed the lights, tension creeping up her back. That was supposed to be Grant up there, wowing the investors. Not *Todd* droning about the benefits of Renewzit, making a blatant pitch for the company. She could swear that a few people in the audience fell asleep.

Fifteen minutes later, as he finally queued the first slide on Midnight Bluff, Mayor Patty stood. "Thank you, Mr. Paxton, that was… enthralling." She edged him from the podium. For a few seconds, he stood at the front of the hall, outrage writ large on his face. Then he stalked to the side of the room.

"I'd like to introduce you to Grant Emberson, Renewzit's representative to Midnight Bluff. Grant has spent the last year with us learning all about the unique history and needs of our town to develop an excellent plan of revitalization for us. The *salient points…*" She glanced at Todd. *"…*from that plan, he will share with you today.

The knots of tension in Ellie's back eased a bit as the investors across the front row sat forward to listen to Grant's presentation.

Grant began, outlining the last couple of decades of Midnight Bluff's decline, from the withdrawal of several manufacturers, the last of which was the catfish plant, to the shrinkage of population and deteriorating school system. Ellie sat in shock. Although she'd helped pull the numbers and relevant info, hearing it laid out so plainly was a dash of reality she hadn't braced for. Picture after picture showed once-thriving streets and happy faces thronging in front of stores where now there was barrenness.

She'd helped craft this presentation but even she was pulled in by Grant's steady, charming oration.

"Midnight Bluff's decline can be traced directly to two main sources. First, the cut-off of the railway line in 1962. With no easy means of transport, manufacturing became unsustainable in the area and national businesses were forced to move to

Chapter 24

larger hubs or even overseas, leaving vacuums in their wake. Second, the rise of modern agriculture, while a huge blessing, has greatly reduced the need for a large, local workforce."

"Without a diversified economy to absorb these blows, Midnight Bluff didn't stand a chance and a systemic population exodus began."

Grant paused to let that sink in, the mood in the room dour, just as they'd planned. He tapped a button, flicking a new image up onto the screen. This one depicted the town square, filled with color, motion, and people.

"But the things that have made Midnight Bluff stumble can now make Midnight Bluff soar." He surveyed the room, his gaze lingering on Ellie. "Where you might see emptiness, I see room to grow. Where you see decay, I see fertile soil." Her heart twisted and pushed against the icy banister encircling it, sending shooting pains through her chest. She crossed her arms, hugging herself while she listened.

For the next few minutes, he walked the investors succinctly through the plans they'd created for Midnight Bluff, from rejuvenating downtown to the series of music and makers' festivals they'd planned. Where her neighbors had looked bored or put off at Grant's proposal of websites and art installations from local craftsmen, their audience nodded along, clearly seeing the vision. The lady in Prada began taking notes at the mention of rural tourism and Dottie wanting to turn her old sharecropper shacks and silos into hip, experience-driven Airbnbs.

But what got everyone's attention was the plan for the co-working space at the catfish plant. Mr. Ernst sat forward in his chair, hands clasped across his stomach and diamond cufflinks twinkling in the low light. As Grant flashed an interior design sketch—where had he gotten that? —up onto the screen, the man began texting on an expensive-looking iPhone, his eyes flicking constantly to the screen while Grant continued.

Grant's face lit up as he animatedly talked over the possibilities for expansion in the space, its interconnectedness with the town, and the plans for the nearby nature trail. Her mind dashed back to their walk through the darkened plant, their kiss.

Heat roared through her body, and she snapped her attention back to the room, blinking at the figures on the projector. Another man next to Mr. Ernst leaned over to whisper something as Grant watched them while explaining the opportunities for lofts above the stores of downtown—easy walking distance.

In the crowd, Herb and Mr. Stevens elbowed each other, grinning. Ellie suppressed a grin of her own. They had them. It was all she could do not to dance in her seat with jubilation at the thought.

Her jubilation lasted until the end of the presentation as Grant finished going through his ten-year projection. As she turned the light back up, the first hand went up.

Mr. Ernst leaned back in his chair. "This is all wonderful. Very thorough plan with a…" He lifted his hands in acknowledgment. "…tempting look into the future." Gesturing at the room and the business owners and townspeople surrounding them, he shook his head. "But you've been here for nearly a year. Why are we just now hearing this proposal?" Ellie fisted her hands as nerves clawed up her throat. "I've done a little digging of my own, and it seems that just now everyone is becoming as gung-ho about this plan as you are."

She wanted to strangle him. She thought this guy would be a sympathetic ear. They'd come so far to have their project

Chapter 24

torpedoed now. But Grant didn't look flustered at all.

He nodded in agreement even. "You're right. There have been some... bumps along the way to get to this stage. I'm not from here, so it took me a while to understand the character of Midnight Bluff and its unique needs. Originally, I tried to give this town a one-size solution when it needed custom-tailoring." Grant winked at Mr. Ernst who guffawed. Todd openly glared at him, making a slashing motion with his hand. Then Grant glanced at Ellie, a smile dancing across his face.

She stared back at him, confused by the personal story. His fingers tightened on the edges of the podium even as the smile froze in place. He continued, voice firm, "But I've made some friends and found someone who opened my heart to everything that this place is and can be. She helped me see Midnight Bluff for what it is. A place to come home to." She bit her lip, trembling. They were just pretty, hollow words—one more selling point.

Mr. Ernst nodded, looking thoughtful. He looked at Mayor Patty. "You've certainly put together an appealing package for us, Patty. You were always good at that." He shrugged. "But all of this..." He hefted the folder. "...is no good if your people aren't behind it. Why should we back any projects in Midnight Bluff?"

Mayor Patty nodded with a beatific smile. "Why don't you speak to them?" She waved at the room, filled with serious faces. Ellie stared at her friends and neighbors, willing them to speak, to defend Grant's plan, and stand behind her faith in the people of Midnight Bluff.

Herb nodded at her, where she stood in the back of the room next to the dimmer switch. "Let Ellie speak. She's talked to us all. She knows us and this plan." Ellie shifted, uncomfortable in her heels which were beginning to rub blisters on her little toes and heels. This wasn't part of what they'd planned. She was there to shake hands and exchange pleasantries. Maybe answer a few questions afterward. She wasn't supposed to speak in front of everyone. Nerves shot through her like electricity through water.

Mayor Patty beckoned her forward impatiently. "Ellie Winters. Our resident real estate expert. She's been helping Mr. Emberson develop our revitalization project the last few weeks."

Grant's hand slid across her back leaving a trail of sparks as she passed him at the podium. Whatever reserve she'd managed to keep went up in flames. A blush worked its way up her neck.

"I ummm... Forgive me. I don't have nearly as much practice at public speaking as Grant... Mr. Emberson... does." She gulped a breath before she could start rambling. Surveying the intent faces of the investors in front of her and the hopeful looks of her neighbors, she began, "I'm just going to say what's on my mind and my heart. I won't repeat any of the points you've already heard. But these last few weeks, I've seen how Gr... Mr. Emberson has striven to make sure this plan meets the needs of this town. He's even taken on a few oddball requests."

Chuckles echoed around the room as Mayor Patty looked down, a little sheepish. "We've met with many of the business owners, many of whom are in this room, to make sure that our goals for infrastructure and the Chamber of Commerce fit their needs. Some have been a bit incredulous with some of our 'window-dressing' as they've called it."

Another rustle of chuckles rippled around the room. "But

Chapter 24

they've come around to the idea." Heads bobbed in agreement. "We can't guarantee exactly how the future will go. No one can. But what I can guarantee is that Midnight Bluff is ready to grow. And I believe in this plan…" She held up the bright red folder. "…and this man." Her eyes captured Grant's, shining in the light as he gazed at her. "And I know that Midnight Bluff is a sure bet because the people who call it home will never give up." Grant's lips trembled, and she turned away.

She nodded as she stepped back from the podium, avoiding Grant's stare. Whistles and claps broke out from her neighbors, filling the room with a cacophony of support.

Looking behind him, Mr. Ernst smiled at the enthusiastic cheers of the crowd, politely adding his claps. Her chest tightened as she took in the other investors' satisfied faces. That cinched it. They had them. Whatever backing they needed for their first stage of development—they would get it.

Mayor Patty beamed at Ellie as she hurried by. There was no need for her to stay now. As the investors pressed forward to talk to Mayor Patty and Grant, she slipped out the back door. Grant could handle any follow-up questions. Why stay longer when it would only rip her heart out to know that she had successfully handed him his ticket out of here?

Eyes blurring, she snatched the heels off her feet and ran.

Chapter 25

Swiping at her eyes trying to clear her vision, Ellie barreled down the steps of the courthouse. Outside, the wind gusted across the square, making the trees tilt and flowers in the sparse beds bob drunkenly. As her eyes filled with fresh tears, she fisted her dress in one hand, praying no one else would be around in case the floaty material decided on some antics of its own.

She dashed into the square and winced. The sun had long since come up, warming the bricks and making them sizzle against Ellie's bare feet. She hopped blindly across them, cursing her decision to park clear across the square at the bakery, but unwilling to slow down to put her shoes back on. A sob worked its way up her throat.

The door behind her thudded open, and she scurried toward the bakery. She didn't want to talk to Mayor Patty or Herb or Mr. Pearce or whoever it was who was coming after her. Not with mascara streaking down her face, and her dress trying to show off just how badly she needed new underwear.

Chapter 25

"Ellie!" Grant's voice rang after her. Nope. No way was she talking to him looking like this. She tried to jog across the scorching bricks. But thanks to her waterlogged vision, an uneven lip caught her big toe, pitching her headlong onto the ground with a startled yep.

Pain lit up her leg as she clutched her foot, bawling. Warm arms encircled her, lifting her from the searing ground and carrying her to a nearby bench. She sniffled and struggled for control as Grant brushed dirt and gravel from her knees, then her palms, tenderly kissing them again and again

"Please, please stop! You're making this worse. You're making it so much worse!" The words burst from her lips in shuddery breaths as he clutched her hands.

"How… How is this worse?" His thumbs swept over the back of her hands, and she snatched them away. Realizing her legs were draped across his lap, she pushed herself upright. Instantly, she longed for the feel of his body against hers.

Ellie buried her face in her hands. "You don't understand. You can't."

He cupped her elbows, his touch searing through her. "What can't I understand? Tell me. I'm trying to help."

"You can't help! You're the problem."

He sat back. "What do you mean? I thought we were…" He gestured between them.

"Just friends?" She laughed bitterly. "How can we be…" Her voice cracked. "…anything when you're leaving?"

"Oh." A laugh shuddered out of him, and he raked a shaky hand through his hair. "I see." He swallowed. "El, I'm not…"

"I know."

He looked at her, eyebrows drawing together. "Know what?"

"You're not…" She gestured to herself. "…into me. Staying.

Whatever. How could you be? You've got a life back in Wisconsin." Trying to flatten her expression, she shrugged. "I get it. I read more into... us... than you meant." She whispered. "I'm not used to casual dating."

"Casua... El. That's not what I'm saying." He shook his head, pressing his lips together.

Gesturing wildly, she stood, spring grass prickly between her toes. "You don't owe me any explanations. No harm, no foul." Finally, this was over, and she could go crawl in a hole and lick her wounds. Preferably with a pint of ice cream and a stack of sitcoms.

"Ellie, will you let me get a word in edgewise?" He stood, waving his arms.

Startled, she looked up at him as he towered over her. He grabbed her shoulders, gently. "I'm not going anywhere." He enunciated the words slowly and stared into her eyes.

Static lit up her brain like snow on a TV screen, the cosmos telling her too much information at once to process. "What... What are you saying?"

She could barely hear him as he said, "Mayor Patty offered me a job. Town planner—I've taken it." He shoved his hands in his pockets as he repeated, "Ellie, I'm staying."

"When did this happen?" Her mouth had gone dry.

"Last week. Mr. Pearce helped me see... And Mr. Tisdale. Well, I've been trying to tell you, but you wouldn't answer my calls, so I figured I'd talk to you today."

Blinking at him, her heart began to beat faster. "But you love the city—"

He shook his head. "Don't you see? You mean more to me than living in a big city, or having lots of money, or even some hotshot career. I just want you, Ellie."

Chapter 25

Her stomach fluttered, begging for this to please, please be real. "I can't ask this of you."

Again, he shook his head as he stepped closer. "You're not. I could never leave you behind. I see that now." He took her hands. "And I'm sorry that I thought it even for a second." Tears burned her eyes as she looked up at him, soaking up his words. "You're the center of my world. And I want to make your home, my home, Ellie. Will you let me do that?"

Ellie swiped at her eyes, determined to absorb every last feature of his face. "Are you sure? Really sure?" Joy eddied up, bubbling from the tips of her toes through her belly to the top of her head as she saw the answer lighting his eyes.

He brushed his thumbs across her cheeks. "I've never been so sure of anything in my life. I love you."

She twined her fingers around the lapels of his suit. "I love you too."

His lips met hers, gentle at first then firmer, harder, desperate to take all of her in and claim her. She parted her lips, and they tasted each other in a heady swirl of tongues, bodies pressed together and hearts beating heavily. His hand cupped the back of her neck, tenderly holding her to him as she clutched his jacket for breathless support.

When they finally parted, nose to nose, and grinning dazed and drunken at each other, a whoop went up behind them. On the courthouse steps crowded most of Midnight Bluff's business owners; Mayor Patty held a handkerchief to her eyes.

"About time, you two!" she called. Todd stood scowling next to her.

Ellie blushed then beamed up at Grant. She slid her hand down into his.

"I take it your current boss doesn't know yet?"

Grant glanced at his watch. "I've got an email scheduled to hit his inbox… right about now."

Ellie laughed. "Such a Grant thing to do." She tugged him towards the truck. "Come on. Let's go home."

Epilogue

Grant watched as Ellie dashed around, her boots echoing on the sealed concrete floors. "Sweetie, I think you can relax. The caterers can handle laying out a few hors d'oeuvres and some sweet tea stations."

"But Mr. Ernst is going to be here any minute and I want—"

"I want you to look relaxed and dignified to meet my guests," Mr. Stevens cut in with a chuckle. "Come on. As my building manager, I insist you come greet people as they arrive and let our more-than-capable friends here…" Willow shot him a grateful look as she and Emma Jean laid out trays. "…do their jobs."

Grant and Mr. Stevens ushered Ellie outside, ducking under the festive ribbon and bow strung across the front, just as the first car crunched over the fresh, new gravel. Mr. Ernst stepped out of his BMW and looked up at the shining façade of PlantedWorx. Down one exterior wall swirled a colorful community mural, a table of spray paint cans nearby.

Mr. Ernst whistled. "If it looks half as good inside as it does

Taken For Granted

out, you did a fine job." He offered a hand to Ellie then to Mr. Stevens and Grant. "I know you've worked tirelessly on this."

A truck rumbled up and Mayor Patty popped out along with her husband, Bob. Ellie smiled at the impish man whose round stature had always reminded her of a walking basketball. He gallantly offered an arm to his wife and escorted her over.

Grant leaned toward her. "Should I do that? Squire you around?"

She swatted his arm. "No. But it wouldn't kill you to open a door for me now and then."

"Noted." He kissed her cheek.

A few minutes later the parking lot was overflowing, cars lining up down the drive as the residents of Midnight Bluff came to celebrate the first new business opening in town in nearly three years.

Grant stared out at the sea of smiling faces, spying a very pregnant looking Cress shepherded by a doting Jake and Leora, Herb plucking at a stiff collar, Al Jr. and Mira with their arms around each other, Dr. Washburn still in scrubs, and Jackie chatting with Vada. Even Mr. Tisdale waved sheepishly to him from the crowd as his kids dodged around people's waists. Mr. Pearce scowled up at him while Lou Ellen at his elbow, with a backpack nonchalantly thrown over her shoulder, gave him a subtle nod.

He tried not to grin.

Most encouraging of all was the dotting of new faces with names he didn't know, many of whom had come from neighboring towns and cities to check out the co-working space and lofts downtown. He made a mental note to make sure they didn't slip away before he had a chance to say hello.

Mayor Patty bustled up, a ridiculously oversized pair of

Epilogue

shears tucked under one arm. "Oh, Ellie dear. We keep getting calls at the courthouse about homes for sale in the area—we have something of a shortage. Anything you can do on that end?"

Grant squeezed Ellie's shoulder as they exchanged a knowing glance. "There's not a lot of existing homes for sale, but Mr. Ernst just introduced me to someone who can help. I'll give him a call in the morning."

"Perfect! Now, where is that photographer..." As Mayor Patty spun off to find her next target, Grant slid an arm around Ellie's waist.

"Serendipitous timing, don't you think?"

She turned in his arms, going up on tiptoe to sneak a kiss. "When you've put the work in, I like to think of it as return on investment."

Stepping away, she began to direct Mr. Ernst and Mayor Patty towards positions in front of the building, the photographer having been successfully located. He flashed Mr. Stevens a thumbs up who in turn winked at the beleaguered photographer.

A ripple of excitement ran through the crowd as Grant flashed another thumbs up at Vada while Ellie's back was turned. Vada and Jackie began poking people into place. At the noise behind her, Ellie turned to see what the hubbub was, but Grant cough noisily into his fist. She turned to him instead, concern creasing her face.

"Are your allergies acting up again?"

He nodded vigorously.

"I'll be right back." She darted under the ribbon and dashed inside.

He looked at the crowd and hissed *hurry*. Everyone quickly

shuffled around each other in seemingly no rhyme or reason but were settled and waiting a few seconds later when Ellie popped back out the door.

Relieved, he accepted the tissue and bottle of water along with the allergy medicine she handed him. "Thanks, sweetie." With an exaggerated honk, he pretended to blow his nose.

Clapping her hands, Ellie turned to everyone and introduced Mr. Stevens and Mr. Ernst. Grant wrapped an arm around her as she stepped back, and together they watched as Mr. Stevens introduced PlantedWorx, the newest business, and the new co-working space come to life, to Midnight Bluff. A moment later, Mayor Patty stepped forward and cut the ribbon in a fanfare of flashing lights and clapping.

Ellie turned to open the doors for the big tour, but Grant grabbed her hand. Mr. Stevens had stepped forward again. "And now a surprise for someone near and dear to all of us."

Heart hammering, Grant pulled her to the front. He clasped her hands in both of his. "Ellie, since the day I met you, you've challenged me to grow and to think about what home and family mean. You know that I want to make Midnight Bluff my forever home."

Lou Ellen skipped forward and handed him the backpack. As he placed it in Ellie's hands, he watched her eyes widen in delight. She admired its sturdy blue canvas and leather straps, the gleaming buckles.

"A new bag!"

He chuckled. "Go on. Open it!"

She unzipped it and peered inside. "Ooh. A laptop pocket!" Laughter rippled through the crowd, and he grinned at them.

"Look a little closer, love," he urged.

As she peered deeper into the bag's dark interior, he sank to

Epilogue

one knee, trembling. When she pulled out the small, red velvet box, her eyes had gone shiny and tremulous. Gently, he took the box and opened it, displaying the ring inside, a princess cut diamond flanked with rubies.

She gasped, the sound barely a whisper, "It's perfect!"

As he slid the delicate ring onto her finger, he asked, "I can think of no better way to ask you to become my wife than surrounded by the town you call family. Ellie, will you marry me?"

Ellie pressed one hand to her mouth then to her heart, choking back tears as she smiled. Looking up, she laughed as she spotted the signs everyone held up spelling, "WILL YOU MARRY ME, ELLIE?"

She looked back down at him and sputtered, "Yes!" Falling to her knees, she planted a kiss on his trembling lips. He wrapped his arms around her, knowing he'd never let her go as long as he lived.

How To Leave A Review

Love this book? Don't forget to leave a review!
Every review matters— and it matters a *lot!*

Head over to Goodreads, BookBub, or wherever you purchased this book to leave a review for:
Taken For Granted: Midnight Bluff Book Two.

Thank you so much for your support.

Mayor Patty's Lemon Bars

Shortbread Crust:
   1 c. – unsalted butter, melted
   ½ c. – granulated sugar
   2 tsp – vanilla extract
   ½ tsp – salt
   2 c. + 2 tbsp – AP flour

Lemon Filling:
   2 c. – granulated sugar
   ½ c– AP flour
   6 – eggs, room temp
   1 ¼ c – fresh lemon juice (about 4 lg lemons)
   Zest of three lemons
   Opt: powdered sugar for dusting

Shortbread Crust Instructions:

1. Heat oven to 350F and line a 9/13 pan with parchment paper, allowing the paper to overlap the edge for easy lifting later.

2. Whisk together flour, salt, and sugar, then pour in the melted butter and vanilla and mix until combined.
3. Sprinkle the dough into your lined pan and press down into a flat, EVEN layer. Bake for 20 minutes or until a light, golden color.

Lemon Filling Instructions:

1. While the crust is baking, add the sugar to a food processor with the zest of 3 lemons. Pulse until zest is fully incorporated—sugar should be a light yellow.
2. Add the sugar and remaining flour to a large bowl and mix well. Pour in the lemon juice and eggs and mix well until completely combined, making sure all flour bits are broken up.
3. Pour the filling onto the warm shortbread crust then bake for 20-25 minutes, turning halfway through, until the center is nearly set and no longer jiggles.
4. Remove from oven and allow to cool for 1 hour. Transfer to refrigerator and chill for 1-2 hours more until chilled through and completely set.
5. Once cooled, carefully lift the parchment paper from the pan. Dust with powdered sugar and cut with a clean, damp knife.

Notes: Cover and store in the refrigerator for up to 1 wk. Freeze individually wrapped in plastic wrap for 3-4 months. If you want to shake things up, substitute grapefruit, blood orange, lime, or orange juice—adjusting your sugar for sweeter juices. Use no less than 1 2/3 c. sugar or the structure of your filling will not come together.

Acknowledgments

Talking with leaders in their fields is one of the greatest pleasures of my writing process and this book has been no exception.

A huge thank you to Gina Smith of Yellow Brick Real Estate for speaking with me at length about the life of a real estate agent. This book also wouldn't be possible without the hospitality of the City of Cleveland—so many locations and events around the city inspired the plot of *Taken For Granted*. They are a shining example of how urban revitalization can work for its citizens.

As always, a huge thank you to my beta readers Abbie, Brenda, Kim, Dawn, and Josh for always being on standby to read my crazy scribblings. You are true rock stars.

To Pete, my always and forever. You cheer me up when I'm stressing out over numbers and due dates, giving me a much-needed dose of reality—and caffeine. Always with the caffeine and Taco Bell. This journey would not be possible without you and I am amazed and humbled every day to have you in my life.

About the Author

Sweet stories with a Southern twang.

Susan Farris is a Mississippi author and poet with a passion for local stories and a deeply held belief that a cup of tea solves many of life's problems. Her favorite local places often appear in her books- along with her favorite foods!

When she's not wrangling words on the page, she loves to garden, play board games, or snuggle up with her menagerie of pets while appreciating her husband's amazing cooking skills.

You can connect with me on:
- https://susanfarris.me
- https://www.facebook.com/SusanFarrisAuthor
- https://www.instagram.com/authorsusanfarris

Subscribe to my newsletter:
- https://susanfarris.me/subscribe